The Murders

Milly Reynolds

ISBN: 1491065087
ISBN-13: 978-1491065082

DEDICATION

To Dave and Matt.

Prologue

Picking up the Rich Tea biscuit between his yellowing finger and thumb, Albert Fisher slowly dipped it into the smooth, silken surface of his eleven o'clock cup of tea. Suddenly, his quiet contemplation was shattered by a piercing scream.

"Pa! Come quick! Our Mabel's running around the garden – naked!"

With a deep sigh, Albert raised his hand and watched as his biscuit dropped, crumb by soggy crumb back into his tea.

"Oh, bugger!"

One

The name's Malone, Detective Inspector Mike Malone. A name of my own choosing, after all, solid alliteration gives that sense of authority that Joe Public seems to like. I had been in this sleepy little town for three months now; three months and I was still waiting for some bombshell to wake the place up – and me. Being a DI can be exciting, exhilarating and energising; it can also be exceedingly, excruciatingly exasperating. However, I had needed this transfer; a change of scene, pace and identity. The Met had been very good to me, letting me go into 'hiding' for a while until everything was forgotten.

It was twelve o'clock and the midday sun was beating through the window onto my desk. Rabbits, dogs and butterflies leapt across my notepad as my fingers entwined to create a menagerie of shadow puppets.

"Sir! Sir!"

Alan Shepherd bounded into my office, scattering the animals into hidden corners. He was bouncing on his toes in excitement.

"A call, Sir. We've got one."

"One what, Shepherd?"

He was quivering with anticipation.

"A case, Sir."

"Well then, Shepherd, lead the way."

Shepherd turned on his heels and scampered out of the office with me in hot pursuit.

Two

The Fisher's cottage might once have stepped off a chocolate box lid. Now however, the whitewash was beginning to peel away from the walls and weeds were invading the cobblestone path. With my trusty Polaroid I took a snap for evidence. Sending Shepherd into the garden to look for clues, I rapped my knuckles on the wooden door to announce my arrival. Hearing nobody say 'go away' I entered and found my way to the small, untidy kitchen.

Doris Fisher was sitting on a stool next to the kitchen table, weeping silently into her pink gingham apron. Her husband, Albert, was sitting by the stove with a bundle of rags on his knee.

"Well, what's the story?" I asked.

Doris Fisher sniffed loudly and the bundle on Albert's knee moved. Two black eyes appeared and watched Doris, puzzled. Doris sniffed again and wrapped her eyes in her hands. No joy there! I turned to Albert who towered above me – and I was standing.

"What did you see?"

The air in the kitchen vibrated as he shook his head violently. Don't these people speak? Looking at the bundle that I assumed was Mabel, even though we hadn't been introduced, I knew that she was one witness that I could not question. So after taking some more snapshots for evidence, I gathered my notebook and nodded a farewell to the Fishers. As I closed the door behind me, flakes of darkness scurried back into the depths of the kitchen as if afraid of the afternoon sun.

Now, where was Shepherd?

Walking to the corner of the cottage I observed
Shepherd on his hands and knees, sniffing the ground.
He always liked to conduct the inch-by-inch
examinations himself, and his techniques, although the
source of amusement to many in the force were usually
very successful. I strode masterfully through the knee
high grasses to join him.

"What can you tell me?"

"Two footprints – one person, Sir."

"And?"

"No sign of a struggle. A quick and clean operation,
Sir."

"Anything else?"

"No, Sir."

I took a couple more snapshots then got out my
notebook. Potatoes, milk, cat food. With my shopping
list complete, I closed the book with a snap – I love that
sound.

"Alright, Shepherd, back to the office. We've got a
crime-board to start."

"Yes, Sir."

With Shepherd once again on two legs, we left the
garden and made our way down the path. As I closed the
gate, I saw out of the corner of my eye three sad pairs of
eyes watching me from the kitchen window.

Three

He watched her as she was enjoying the feel of the afternoon sun on her back. A blue lady had just landed on the bush in front of her and was stretching out its wings. She was watching the tiny creature, transfixed.

She didn't hear his gentle footsteps approaching her. In fact she was so spellbound by the little blue lady that she heard nothing at all. She only felt the touch of cold steel on her back, and then – it was too late.

We had our crime-board. I was amazed that no one here had ever used one before; in London I found them invaluable, being able to see all of the evidence in one place and finding the links. After lots of hammering it was eventually fastened to the wall in front of my desk and Shepherd was watching me, waiting for me to pass on my wisdom.

Laying all of the photos that I had taken at the Fisher's place out on my desk, I studied them to see if I could make some sort of sense of this senseless crime. I couldn't. Maybe if I pinned them to the board things would become clearer.

"Hand me the drawing pins, Shepherd."

"Yes, Sir."

Mabel's photo had to go in the centre of the board; she was the victim. Doris had given me one of her that was taken at last summer's show. I pinned the photos of Albert and Doris Fisher above her and the house and garden underneath. Arrows! Crime-boards need arrows – but where to put them. This case was baffling. The arrows were leading nowhere.

At the sound of the telephone, I dropped the arrows onto the threadbare carpet. Drat! Shepherd answered the call and I watched him as his face became animated. He put the phone down and turned to face me.

"Another one, Sir!"

"Same as Mabel?"

"Yes, Sir!"

Leaving the arrows scattered under my desk until later, I picked up my jacket and led the way out of the office towards my car. Two very similar cases in a very short space of time. It looked as if we had a serial criminal on the loose.

As the door closed behind us the little arrows fluttered in the breeze until they all pointed south.

Four

In a cellar ten miles to the south of the town, a second white fleece was placed gently into a crate.

Fred and Betty Greengrass looked on in embarrassment as Emily danced across the manicured lawn, revelling in her nakedness.

"Come on in, lass. Let's get you covered up." Fred was frantic with worry.

As I watched I could see Shepherd, on all fours again, approaching her. As she twirled on her toes, he crouched behind her and waited. Sensing his presence, Emily gambolled into the parlour where Fred swept her up into his arms while Betty threw a blanket over her. As for me, I was hoping that this time I might get some answers, or if I was very lucky, a lead. After all, this time I had actually heard someone speak.

"So, Fred. Can you tell me what happened?"

"No!"

"Didn't you see or hear anything?"

The silence deafened me. Here we go again! I turned to Betty.

"Did you see anything?"

Betty lifted her head, shook it quickly, and ran from the room. Once again the only witness was one who was unable to give me answers. From the comfort of Fred's lap, Emily raised her head, looked straight at me and chewed slowly. I felt the kettle in my brain click on and the steam begin to rise. This was so frustrating! Before the kettle had chance to boil I left the cottage to go and find Shepherd.

Opening the garden gate, I was surprised to see that Shepherd was on two feet; he had already finished his search.

"Found anything?"

"Same as last time. Two footprints, Sir."

I was about to close my notebook with that satisfying snap when I spotted the look on Shepherd's face. This cat had got the cream.

"What else, Shepherd?"

"A blond eyelash, Sir. It was on a blade of grass next to the footprints."

"Well done, Shepherd. This could be the breakthrough that we are looking for."

This time when I closed my notebook with a satisfying snap, I was doubly satisfied. The eyelash was safely between its pages. Leaving Shepherd to take the photos for the crime-board, I rushed back to the office to contemplate the clue.

Five

Back in the office I considered what had been discovered so far about this strange crime wave that seemed to be sweeping the town. Firstly, two defenceless ewes, from different parts of the town, had been stripped of their wool. Secondly, the evidence so far seemed to suggest that these attacks were being carried out by someone working alone. Thirdly, the wool thief had left behind a vital clue – an eyelash which was nestling between the pages of my notebook at this very moment. It was a vital clue, but I needed to know so much more. For instance – why was the wool so important?

"Sir, I've got the photos for you."

I looked up to see Shepherd at the door with several glossy photographs clasped in his hand like a fan. He must have run all the way from the Greengrass cottage; his cheeks were a delicate pink and his sandy hair was windswept. I sighed. In a certain light he reminded me of my ….

"Sir, I've got the photos."

"Well, bring them here, lad, and let's add them to the crime-board."

Carefully I pinned the photo of the most recent victim, Emily, near Mabel's photo. Next, the photos of Fred and Betty, the cottage, and finally the footprints. I stood back to admire my work.

"So, Shepherd. What links these two crimes?"

"Both victims are sheep, Sir."

"Well done! Now where's my arrow?"

During my visit to the Greengrass residence, Nellie had been in to clean and the arrows had been picked up and stacked neatly on the corner of my desk. I picked the top one up and pinned it to show the link between Emily and Mabel. As I did so, something caught my eye.

"Shepherd, my ruler."

Shepherd handed me my twelve inch and I started examining the two photos of the footprints.

"We are looking for one man – or woman, Shepherd. Look at this. Both footprints are exactly one and one quarter inch in length. They are identical. Both crimes were committed by the same person. So …"

Sitting down and taking a slide rule from the right hand drawer of my desk, I did a few quick calculations.

"Scaling the photos up to correct size, we are looking for someone with size nine and a half feet. As I don't know any women with feet that large, I deduce that we are looking for a man."

Admiration was evident in Shepherd's eyes and I basked in its light, like a seal soaking up the warmth of the sun's rays. Taking a sheet of paper, I quickly drew a quick identikit of the person we were looking for. A man with a shoe size of nine and a half. Not a lot to go on at the moment, but with the second clue of the eyelash, well, the picture would soon be complete.

"Now to see what this guy looks like."

Shepherd watched me intently as I unlocked my battered filing cabinet and it made my heart swell when I heard him gasp as I removed my pride and joy. The light reflected off the gleaming silver surface of the microscope. This had been a present from a very grateful scientist a few years ago – but that is another story for another time.

"Clear the desk, Shepherd and let's get this baby up and running."

Shepherd carefully removed my blotter and the arrows and I set the microscope down carefully in the centre of the desk. Opening the second drawer in my desk, I removed a couple of slides.

"No breathing, lad. Can't have this vital piece of evidence escaping."

Scarcely breathing myself, I removed my notebook from my jacket pocket. Opening it carefully I extracted the delicate eyelash, placed it on the centre of one of the slides and sealed it with the second.

"Now to see who you are."

Placing the slide on the microscope, I switched on the light and lowered my eye. Everything swam out of focus and it took some careful turning of the knob to bring the eyelash into clear view. Perfect! This baby sure was delicate. It curved slightly at the tip and was the colour of pure gold. I looked up at Shepherd, satisfied.

"Come and have a look, lad"

Shepherd needed no second invitation. He leapt across the room and with shaking hands he embraced the microscope as he looked down.

"Wow!"

"Exactly! We can now say that our criminal has natural blond hair. He may be dying his hair as a disguise, but he has not dyed his eyelashes. They remain a pure blond. So – take this down, Shepherd – we are looking for a male with size nine and a half feet, with dark or blond hair, but crucially with blond eyelashes."

"The net is closing, Sir."

"In the morning we will issue a description and visit all the townspeople to see if they know anyone matching this description. Have an early night, Shepherd – we have a busy day tomorrow."

"Yes, Sir. Good-night, Sir."

Shepherd left the office and after carefully replacing the microscope and ensuring that the eyelash was safely under lock and key, I left the station.

Six

It was twenty six minutes past six when I locked my green Ford Mondeo and walked up the path to my cottage. In the front window, Ophelia sat waiting for me, rubbing her nose against the glass in greeting. As soon as I unlocked the front door, she leapt from the windowsill and wrapped herself around my ankles.

"Hi, girl! Did you miss me?"

Ophelia meowed loudly and continued to wind herself around my legs. I walked in to the kitchen and she sat next to her bowl, looking hopeful. I knew there would be no peace until she had eaten so, opening a tin of chopped rabbit, I let the sloppy mess squelch into her bowl. Immediately sounds of happy slurping filled the kitchen.

As for me, I needed something with a little more style.

I have always prided myself upon my culinary skills; my food is as good as, if not better than, the food served in many restaurants. So, after some chopping, slicing and frying my meal was ready. A sprinkling of freshly grated parmesan was all that was needed to complete my masterpiece. Magnificent!

Later, with the washing-up completed, Ophelia and I retired to the lounge so that I could indulge myself with my second love – William Shakespeare. Tonight Shylock was going after his pound of flesh while unfortunately, my own serial criminal was probably after his pound of wool.

The constant chiming of the telephone interrupted my dreams. Momentarily, I was slightly unsure of my whereabouts. Only seconds before I had been gazing across the Grand Canal, watching Bassanio depart on his gift-laden barge. Now, I was back on my old, familiar leather sofa, with Ophelia curled up across my stomach like a leaden weight. Trying not to disturb her dreams, I reached across for the telephone.

"Malone."

"It's Shepherd, Sir. There's been another fleecing. This one has turned nasty."

"Whereabouts?"

"Samuel Spicer's, Sir, in Long Row."

"I'll meet you there."

Looking at my watch as I replaced the receiver, I saw that it was 3.30am. My serial criminal had changed his pattern of operation. Emily and Mabel had been attacked in daylight. The latest assault was during the hours of darkness. Was he trying to throw me off the scent?

I gently caressed Ophelia to awaken her and then stretched myself into wakefulness. As I did so Ophelia watched me with a mixture of annoyance and affection. At least I think it was affection. Do cats ever love their owners as much as we love them? Grabbing my mackintosh – it was bound to be cold outside – I left the warmth of my cottage, blowing Ophelia a kiss as I closed the door behind me.

Surprisingly, it was a pleasant drive to the Spicer's. The moon was almost full and the earth was covered with a shimmering light. It was as if everything had been covered with fairy dust; magic was in the air. I almost expected to see Titania and her group of fairies flitting across the fields.

Shepherd was standing outside the Spicer's cottage when I arrived. He approached as I pulled up and bending slightly, he opened my door.

"Well, Shepherd?"

"Felicity Spicer, Sir. She was in the outside barn. Fleeced like the others. However, she put up a fight. He cut her, Sir, several times. Nothing serious but she is very distressed - the vet's with her now."

"Do you think that she managed to cut him?"

"Difficult to say, Sir. There are traces of what could be skin on her hoof."

"Excellent! Get it bagged and sent to the lab as soon as possible."

Shepherd led the way into the Spicer's cottage where the aroma of cigarette smoke and coffee surrounded me immediately. I looked around at the yellowing, nicotine stained wallpaper. An unhealthy environment if ever I saw one.

Samuel Spicer and his wife, Judy, were in the lounge. Samuel was a short, blustering man in his fifties; his cheeks were puffing up and down like a pair of bellows. Judy, on the other hand, was sitting meekly at the corner of the hearth watching her husband intently, afraid to make a sound in case his frustration should blow up in her direction.

"Mr Spicer – Detective Inspector Mike Malone. What can you tell me?"

The explosion was ferocious.

"What can I tell you? It's you who should be telling me! My taxes pay your wages, my lad. You should be protecting my Felicity, not allowing some madman to

19

cut her to ribbons. So, sonny, what can you tell me?"

The debris from the blast floated down upon us; in fact Judy now appeared to have turned quite grey.

"Mr Spicer, I quite understand your distress. I want to catch this person as badly as you want me to catch him. However, to do that I need your help. I need you to tell me every little detail about what happened here tonight, no matter how small and insignificant it might seem. Will you help me?"

"There's nothing to tell. It was only Felicity crying that woke us up. Can't tell you anything."

Samuel Spicer flopped down into his battered armchair – the explosion had left him exhausted. Saying goodbye, Shepherd and I left the cottage and walked across to the barn.

The vet stood as we entered. I immediately noticed that he was tall and blond. Glancing at his wellingtons, I wondered about his shoe size; was he perhaps size nine and a half? Better check his eyes. As I approached to offer my hand I gazed directly into his blue eyes. In fact I gazed into the deep blue pools for so long that he turned quite red with embarrassment and looked away. He definitely had blond eyelashes, but the compassion and kindness that shone out of him told me that not only was I barking up the wrong tree, I was in the wrong flipping forest!

'DI Mike Malone. Nasty business." I shook his hand firmly.

"It certainly is. Dan Marshall, pleased to meet you." He turned away and knelt again to tend to his patient.

I gasped when I looked down at the sad form of

Felicity lying on the soft straw. Like the other two victims, she was naked, but unlike the others, there were nasty cuts across her shoulders and back where she had been snipped as she had struggled to escape her attacker.

"Has the skin from her hoof been bagged?"

The vet handed me a small polythene envelope.

"How is she?" I asked.

"I've given her a sedative. The cuts look worse than they actually are. Physically she'll be as right as rain, but mentally? Trauma of this kind affects everyone in different ways. She'll be needing plenty of TLC."

I nodded my thanks and, patting Felicity gently, Shepherd and I left the barn.

"Well, Shepherd – did you get any clues this time? I assume you have plenty more photos for the board?"

"Plenty, Sir. And, a new clue. Lying beside Felicity in the hay there was a metal button. The Spicers don't recognise it."

"Excellent! Let's get back to the station and examine it carefully."

"I'll meet you there, Sir."

Shepherd and I parted at the cottage gate. I returned to my car and set off, marvelling at both the golden light that was beginning to decorate the horizon, and the horrific cruelty of man.

Seven

A blue van pulled up on the river bank. The driver got out and slowly walked down to the river's edge where he busied himself with the task of filling his jacket pockets with stones. Once he was satisfied that every pocket was as full as it could be, he removed his jacket and wrapped it into a tight bundle. Drawing his arm back, he threw the jacket as far as he could into the middle of the river. Sadly, he watched the blue denim spread across the tranquil water and then, slowly, sink from view. That jacket had been his pride and joy. What a fool he had been to lose that button!

Shepherd had been in the office nearly half an hour when I arrived. I had needed to go for a drive to calm the growing anger that was threatening to explode inside me. Mindless violence and cruelty always affected me in this way. I had wanted a bombshell to liven up this little town, but this was turning into a blood-letting. I was not a happy man.

"I've completed the board, Sir."

Shepherd was standing before the crime-board. If it wasn't for the savagery behind the pictures, you could almost say that it was a work of art. Delicate gold threads were entwined around the red arrows that linked victim to victim; family to family; clue to clue.

I sat down at my desk and removed my magnifying glass.

"The button, Shepherd."

Shepherd gingerly removed the little plastic envelope

containing the metal button from his inside pocket and handed it to me. With a pair of tweezers I carefully grasped the button and held it up for closer examination.

"Levi Strauss. This could only have come from a denim jacket. Any ideas, Shepherd?"

"Well, Sir, denim is traditionally worn by the younger generation. Our chap must be around my age."

"Perhaps, but what about the older generation who wear denim jackets to try and recapture their youth? What about the middle-aged man who is trying to hold back the tides of time?"

"Do you have a denim jacket, Sir?"

"Of course not!" I spluttered, thinking of the jacket hidden at the back of my wardrobe. I could feel my cheeks beginning to redden under Shepherd's mischievous grin. He looked as pleased as a schoolboy who has just caught his teacher smoking behind the bike-shed. I had to re-establish my credibility, and quickly.

"So, we may not be able to guess the age of this man, but we can start to think like him. So, Shepherd, hypothesize. You have lost a button whilst committing a most heinous crime. What do you do?"

"Do, Sir?"

"Yes – do. What do you do with the jacket?"

"Oh, see what you mean. Well, I wouldn't keep it. It would be too conspicuous with a button missing."

"Yes! Exactly! This button may be a clue – but it's useless. The jacket would have been disposed of immediately. Our chap is too smart to have kept it."

"So, what do we do now, Sir?"

"Keep looking, lad, keep looking."

I put the magnifying glass back into my desk drawer and sighed. This case was going nowhere. Nothing but dead-ends. Shepherd sensed my mood.

"Breakfast, Sir. It's 5.30 and the local café will be open now."

"Good idea, lad. A good breakfast will shed a whole new light on things."

Eight

We had hardly had chance to digest our excellent English breakfast before the next bombshell hit. Another attack and this one was even worse than the last. This guy was becoming sadistic.

Arriving at Jim Wallace's farm, we saw the horror for ourselves. Not a single sheep this time. Oh no – our guy was getting brazen. This time he had attacked five innocent ewes. He had forced them to watch as he had stripped them one after the other, snipping and cutting their delicate skin as he had done so. When he had fleeced Mabel and Emily, he had been caring and gentle as he violated them. Now he was making sure that the deed was done as quickly as possible, and if the victim got hurt in the process – so be it. He no longer cared.

I left Shepherd to take the photos and to comb the ground for clues in his usual manner. As for me – I was unable to look upon the pain, bewilderment and fear in the eyes of the five victims. I turned away and set off to find Jim and his family.

The farmhouse was a slice of heaven after the hell of the sheep field. Jim and his wife, Moira, were in the kitchen. Moira handed me a steaming hot cup of tea and I sat down by the Aga cuddling it gratefully. After what I had just witnessed in the field, I decided that maybe my usual line of questioning was not appropriate. I needed to be softer.

"So, did either of you see or hear anything?"

Jim and Moira exchanged glances. Not glances of the guilty. These were glances that conveyed confusion and horror at the pitiful scene outside in the field.

"Nothing, I was in the cowshed. Early milking. Can't hear anything once the pumps start."

Moira blew into her cup to cool her tea.

"I was collecting eggs from the hen-house. It's on the far side of the yard. The farmhouse blocks out the view of the fields from there. Sorry, I'm not being much help, am I?" A tear rolled down her cheek and dropped silently into the mug.

"That's no problem. This guy is clever. This is the fourth attack and there are still no real clues."

"I have one."

We all turned towards the voice that was descending the staircase. We watched as two pink feet, a blue nightie and then the tousled head of Jim and Moira's nine year old daughter came into view.

"Jenny, love – don't go bothering the policeman. He's very busy." Moira put a protective arm around her daughter.

"But I saw something, Mum. I was at the window watching the sunrise and I saw a blue van in the lane near the sheep field. It didn't have its lights on."

My heart leapt into the air, performed a quick backward somersault and then perfected a perfect landing.

"Are you sure?" I was getting excited. "You definitely saw a blue van?"

"Yes – like the post van, but blue."

"Jenny – you have been an enormous help. Thank you." I turned back to Jim and Moira. "Do either of you know anyone who drives a blue van?"

"Sorry, no one." Jim shook his head,

"No matter. This is our first important clue. Thanks."

I handed my mug back to Moira and left to find Shepherd – there were house-to-house enquiries to start.

By 4.30pm Shepherd and I had visited every farm, house and business premises in the town. Nothing! No one knew anything of a blue van. It was unbelievable! A community of this size and not one blue van, not even a blue car or bike. What was wrong with blue? This was hopeless. Every clue was leading to a locked door. For the first time in my career I was feeling useless and I didn't like it.

Shepherd had his back to me and was examining the crime-board. I studied him in silence; the strong shoulders, the way his hair curled over his collar. He reminded me so much of my …

"Sir!"

I quickly turned my attention back to my notepad where I had been contemplating the uses that anyone could have for so much wool. So far I had come up with two jumpers, three pairs of socks and a scarf!

"Sir, I've had a thought. Look at the addresses of the attacks. They are all quite difficult to find. These are not opportunistic crimes. This chap has planned them carefully. He has deliberately chosen farms that are off the beaten track."

"So?"

"So he might be someone who lives here – or – he might be someone who used to live here. However, if he were living here now someone would know him – and

27

his blue van. So – he must have left sometime ago – and he must bear the town a grudge."

"You could have a point, Shepherd. You know these people better than me. You speak their language. Ask around. Has anyone left recently under a cloud? Has anyone left in a thunderstorm?"

"Will do, Sir."

"But not now. Start in the morning, Shepherd. Let's go home, we've had a long day."

"See you in the morning, Sir."

"Goodnight, Shepherd."

Nine

By the time I reached my cottage, my depression had deepened. The victims were piling up and I was no nearer to solving the case. How many more were going to have to suffer so that he could satisfy his lust for wool? And, why was he collecting all of this wool? Was he intending to open up a woolly jumper shop? Did he have a shed full of old ladies with their knitting needles at the ready?

Ophelia rubbed herself against my legs but even she could not help my mood tonight. I had come to this sleepy town three months ago to try and banish my demons and kill my devils. I had been succeeding, but now the innocent were once again suffering before my eyes.

Food, I needed food. It seemed so long ago since that beautiful English breakfast. I needed something quick and satisfying. A splash of oil, some sizzling tomatoes and hey presto! A bowl of steaming pasta to settle the grumblings in my stomach.

Ophelia accompanied me into the lounge and we sat companionably together. Every now and then she would sneak a piece of pasta off my plate with her paw when she thought that my attention was elsewhere. When we had both finished, I stretched myself out upon the sofa. No Shakespeare tonight; my mind could not concentrate upon his wondrous phrases. Instead Ophelia and I lay in silence and watched the moonlight playing over the fields; dark shadows moved slowly across the sky. Then I noticed it! The stars were twinkling! They were giggling and pointing at me because I had not caught this chap. I'd like to see them do my job! With a snap, I closed the curtains.

Ten

The blue van, its lights switched off, rolled silently into the High Street and stopped outside the police station. The male occupant descended and went around the vehicle to open the back door. Using a tail-lift, he gently lowered a large crate into position outside the doors to the station. After gazing upon his art work for a few moments with a sense of satisfaction, he quietly closed the back doors and returned to the driver's seat. Keeping the van in darkness, he quietly crept away.

Rolling over, I picked up the phone, at the same time glancing at my alarm clock which was standing to attention. Five o'clock!

"Malone."

"It's Grayson, Sir. Sorry to call you so early but you had better come down to the station." I sat up. Grayson had thirty years service behind him. For him to call me, something serious must have happened, or if it hadn't, I would want to know why not.

"What is it, Grayson?"

"Wool, Sir."

"Wool?"

"All the fleeces, Sir. They've all been delivered to the station."

"Give me half an hour."

I turned back the duvet and put my feet onto the soft carpet. This case was getting stranger by the minute. Why was he returning the wool? Was it the wrong colour?

I pulled up at the station and gazed at the curious sight before my eyes. In the middle of the yard there was a large wooden crate stuffed with fleeces; white wool was trying to squeeze itself free through the slats in the sides. Why? Why go to all the bother of fleecing those poor creatures just to leave the evidence here? Was he mad?

Grayson appeared on the steps and rushed down to open my door.

"We've not touched anything, Sir. We waited for you."

"Good man."

"Did you want us to call Shepherd, Sir?"

"No, leave him. He's on duty at seven. We can deal with this."

I walked around the crate taking care not to touch the sides and contaminate the evidence. The fleeces were laid flat one upon the other – but – something was not quite right. I made some calculations on my fingers. Eight fleeces – each roughly three to four inches deep – should make a pile of around two feet. This crate was a good three feet in height. The fleeces should not be nearing the top of the crate – but they were! Something was in the crate with them!

"Grayson! Bring me some rubber gloves and get a pair for yourself. We need to remove these fleeces."

While I was waiting, I removed a plastic sheet from the boot of my car and laid it on the ground beside the crate. Grayson returned and once we were equipped, we set to work.

With great care, we removed the first fleece. I was surprised by its weight. Shouldn't wool be light? After all my jumper weighs next to nothing. I decided that being brought up in the city might have equipped me for many things, but an understanding of farm animals was not one of them. We laid the fleece on the sheet and turned our attention to the second one in the pile. Within minutes it too was laid upon the sheet.

As Grayson placed his hand upon the third fleece, he gasped.

"Sir, there's a hand!"

I hurried round to join Grayson. He lifted the corner of the third fleece and there it was. A human hand! Not just a hand; lifting the fleece further we could see that the third fleece was infact providing a funeral shroud for a corpse. The corpse was a grey-haired gentleman in his fifties. A gentleman with a kindly face and wearing wire-rimmed spectacles. A gentleman who could just have climbed into the crate and fallen asleep, if it had not been for the vivid purple bruises on his throat. Bruises that had crushed his windpipe and deprived him of life. My sheep-shearing friend had turned his hand to murder! Damn him!

"My God, it's Sir Jonathon Black!" Grayson stammered, his face as white as the dead man's.

"And he is?"

"He lives in Elderton Manor, the large house just outside town. But he wouldn't harm a fly. He's – was - an eccentric old chap. Likes trying to invent things to help the local farmers – self-filling food troughs and automatic brooms – that sort of thing. Always giving money to charity. He's harmless. Who'd want to kill him? Oh, Sir! I've just remembered."

"What, lad?"

"He's Alan Shepherd's godfather – he and his wife brought him up. The boy's devoted to him."

"Right, get the medical guys to remove the body and I'll deal with Shepherd."

With a nod Grayson left to make all of the appropriate phone calls. I looked at the face of Jonathon Black. Grayson was right. This was the face of a gentle gentleman. I carefully bent down and examined his hands and neck. No sign of rope marks. Well, he hadn't been tied up. I brushed aside the grey hair from his collar, and there it was. Just above the purple bruise, a puncture mark. He had been drugged. Then he had been taken to his place of execution and strangled before being packed up and delivered to me. But why wrap him in wool? Why not use black bags, like normal murderers? There had to be a connection between the wool and the murder – but what?

The sound of vehicles pulling up alerted me to the arrival of the medical team. Briefing them on the need to remove the body to the mortuary as quickly as possible, I checked my watch. Six fifteen. Good! I had time to go and catch Shepherd before he set off for the station.

Eleven

It took just under ten minutes to get to Shepherd's cottage. I didn't know a lot about his family life except that he lived alone. His parents had died when he was a child and he had been looked after by a friend of the family, a friend I now knew to be Jonathon Black. His close relationship with the Blacks was probably the reason why he had chosen to remain in this sleepy little town instead of seeking the bright lights of the city.

I knocked softly on the door. I could hear footsteps on the stairs and the door opened. Shepherd had not yet put on his blue police shirt. Looking at his smooth chest and his uncombed hair, he seemed like a boy of 14 instead of a young man of 24. Such youthful innocence and I was going to destroy it.

"Hello, Sir. Er – is something wrong?" He looked at his watch. "I'm sure that I'm not due to start till seven today."

Even his confusion was child-like.

"Can I come in, lad? I need to talk to you."

Shepherd stepped back to let me into the cottage. As he closed the door, he grabbed his shirt off the banister and put it on. Leading the way into the lounge he motioned me to sit. I glanced around and spotted two large photographs on the wall. Shepherd noticed my interest.

"My parents, Sir. They were taken shortly after they were married. Mum always said that she would have liked proper portraits of her and Dad – huge oil things that would last generations. The photos were the nearest they got." He smiled at the memory.

"It must have been awful for you when they died?"

"I was eight. They were killed in a boating accident. Aunt Helen took me in and I've lived here in this part of Lincolnshire ever since."

"Aunt Helen was your mother's sister?"

"Oh, no! Mum and Dad were both only children – I didn't even have any real aunts and uncles. Aunt Helen and Mum had gone to school together. They'd been really close friends. I used to visit her and Uncle Jon in the school holidays and so it was just natural that I lived with them after the accident."

I nodded. Now for the part of my job that I always hated.

"I take it that Uncle Jon is Sir Jonathon Black?"

"Yes, but …?"

"I'm sorry, lad. I've some bad news. I'm afraid that your uncle has been murdered."

Shepherd's face drained of colour and crumpled like a tissue. I moved over to the sofa and sat beside him; he seemed so young and vulnerable.

"Can I fetch you a glass of water, lad?"

He sniffed loudly and shook his head. He was trying desperately to hold back the tears.

"Does Aunt Helen know?"

"No – I came to see you first. I didn't want you hearing from one of the lads when you arrived at the station. I wanted to tell you myself."

"Thank you, Sir. Wh … what happened?"

"Looks as if it's our guy. Your uncle was left outside

the station, wrapped in the stolen fleeces."

"Oh my God!" Shepherd's valiant battle was over and burying his head in his hands he succumbed to rasping sobs. I put my arm around his shoulders.

"Let it out, lad, you'll feel calmer. When you're ready, I'll drive you to your Aunt Helen's and we'll tell her together."

Shepherd's shoulders shuddered a reply.

Twelve

Twenty minutes later we were in my car heading towards Elderton Manor. I had given Shepherd time off and without his uniform he looked just like a schoolboy playing truant, except of course for his pallor and red rimmed eyes. He was huddled down into his seat almost as if he was physically trying to hold himself together. I turned my head towards him.

"We will get him. You do know that, don't you?"

Shepherd raised his head and looked at me through red swollen eyes. Even more now could I see that shy little schoolboy.

"It would have been their thirtieth wedding anniversary next month. I've been organising a surprise party" Shepherd's fist slamming into dashboard surprised me with its ferocity – I almost jammed on the brakes, it was so unexpected. "He didn't deserve this, Sir, he didn't."

"I know, lad, I know. Look, I've got to ask this, but do you know of anyone who would have wanted to harm your uncle?"

Shepherd put his head back on the leather seat.

"No – everyone seemed to like him. They all thought he was a bit mad – eccentric, but he wouldn't hurt a fly."

"That's just what Grayson said."

"How did he … I mean, did he … ?"

"He was strangled, lad. I can't say until I get the report, but I think he was drugged first. I'm pretty sure that there was a puncture mark on his neck."

"That doesn't make any sense."

"Maybe because the murderer wanted to kill him well away from where he was taken. I can't say more than that, lad. Maybe when the lab tells us what type of drug was used, it will be clearer."

Shepherd shrugged and we continued in silence for the next few minutes, each of us lost in our own thoughts.

"Next right, Sir. You'll see a set of iron gates."

I nodded and seconds later I was turning into a tree lined drive. Following the roadway round, the house suddenly appeared before me almost as if the trees had parted like curtains on a stage to reveal a fantasy backdrop. However, for all its grandeur, there was a homely air about the house. In fact the windows seemed to be twinkling mischievously as if they were hiding a secret and the front door was gaping open as if in welcome. I could see that two chocolate brown Labradors were playing hide and seek in the bushes. A perfect scene and here was I to spoil it. There were times when my job seemed cruel, and this was one of them.

I eased the car to a halt and put my hand on Shepherd's shoulder.

"Ready, lad?"

He nodded.

"Do you want to tell her yourself, or do you want me to?"

Shepherd made no reply, he just blinked his eyes furiously to try to keep the tears at bay. I squeezed his shoulder and opened my door. Immediately the two dogs stopped their game and came rushing over, tails wagging excitedly. As I got out wet noses were pushed into my hands in welcome. Some guard dogs these were!

39

When Shepherd emerged the dogs deserted me and rushed at him, leaping all over him in greeting. I watched as he grabbed them and buried his face in their warm coats, trying to take some small crumbs of comfort. Their three bodies merged as if to create a strange garden sculpture – a perfect representation of comfort and grief. Finally he released the dogs and with a slight glance in my direction he led the way into the house.

"Aunt Helen," he shouted, "it's Alan. Where are you?"

"In the lounge, dear."

Shepherd led me towards the voice and we went into the second room off the entrance hall. A small figure was kneeling at the fireplace, arranging flowers in a large oriental vase. As she turned towards us, my breath was taken away by her fragility. Wow! Blonde hair curled around her face, as if it wanted to protect her from harm; her blue eyes shone with kindness, gentleness and joy and her skin seemed almost translucent, like the most delicate porcelain. But it was her smile that broke my heart, a smile of such radiance. I knew then that in a few short seconds I would destroy it; it would never be seen again.

In fact my very presence was already causing it to diminish.

"Alan, dear, why are you here? Shouldn't you be at work? Has something happened? Who is your friend?"

Fear was drawing a blind over those blue eyes; their brilliance was beginning to fade. Shepherd went over to her and helped her to her feet. As soon as she looked into his eyes, fear flooded her face. He led her to the

40

crumpled cream sofa.

"Alan? What is it?"

Shepherd opened his mouth but the words that would break his aunt's heart refused to be spoken. He looked pleadingly at me as he enveloped her in his arms,

"Lady Black," I stammered. "I'm sorry to have to bring you this bad news but I'm afraid that the body of your husband was found early this morning. He…"

Before I could finish she had collapsed into Shepherd's chest and her sobs were threatening to tear her tiny frame into two.

"Sir, please, can we have a moment?"

I nodded. Just before I left the lounge, I glanced over my shoulder and saw Shepherd and his aunt clinging to each other, desperately trying to protect each other from further harm.

Turning right out of the lounge, I quickly discovered the kitchen.

Thirteen

The Black's kitchen was exactly as I had expected it to be; warm and homely. A large green Aga was nestled into one corner and an old pine Welsh dresser took pride of place in another. Every inch of its surface was covered with a family memento. There were photos of Shepherd in his police uniform and photos of the three of them together. I picked up a battered silver frame and looked intently at the faces staring back at me. It had been taken on a beach not long ago and Shepherd was standing between Sir Jonathon and his wife. The bright smiles and the laughing eyes showed that this was indeed a happy family. Why did someone want to destroy it? What motive was there? Why would someone want to murder a man who seemed perfectly harmless?

Replacing the frame I looked at the others. Many were of Shepherd as a boy; there was a lovely one of him at around the age of five with a friend. The pair of them were grinning widely to show off their missing front teeth. Thankfully, Shepherd's looks had improved with age. In every photo there was a sense of an idyllic family life. People always say that the kitchen is the heart of the family. That was evident here, their very heart and soul was captured on that dresser; a heart that had now been cruelly broken.

I sat at the pine table and began to tap my fingers. The echo of skin on wood seemed suddenly out of place in this house of sorrow – too cheerful. I stopped and walked over to the window. In the garden the dogs were busy chasing butterflies. Hadn't they even missed their master? I felt useless in the midst of so much heartache.

Tea! The English solution to everything. I decided to make a cup of tea. After looking around, in and on top of cupboards I soon located everything that I needed and in 10 minutes I was re-entering the lounge, tray in hand.

The first wave of grief had passed. Shepherd and Lady Black were sitting holding hands and talking quietly as I entered. Lady Black raised her head and gave me a watery smile.

"Tea, I thought it would do us all good."

Once we were all equipped with a china cup and saucer, I decided to try and ask a few questions.

"Lady Black, I know this is incredibly difficult for you but I do need to ask you some questions. If it is too much for you today, I can return tomorrow."

"No – that's fine. Alan said that you would want to talk to me." She squeezed Shepherd's hand gratefully.

"I've already asked … er, Alan this, but do you know of anyone who might have wanted to harm your husband?"

"No one at all. He was always helping people and he made regular large donations to local charities."

"OK." I scribbled notes in my book. "I'm sorry but I must ask this, who inherits the title?"

"No one – it dies with him. He will be the last ever .." She removed a white silk handkerchief from her sleeve and wiped her eyes. "We never had any children of our own, you see."

"So, … who inherits the estate, the money?"

"I do. The entire estate goes to me."

"And after your death?"

I almost heard the snap in Shepherd's neck as he spun his head around to face me, His eyes shot daggers at my audacity in asking such a question.

"It's alright, Alan. He has to ask. Alan will inherit everything after my death. It's no secret."

"So am I a suspect, Sir?" Shepherd's face was flushed with a mixture of annoyance and grief. I hated to see him like this and hoped desperately that when everything was calmer we could return to our normal working relationship, the one where he admired everything that I did.

"Of course not, lad. But it's my job to ask – you should know that."

I had to look away from him and I decided to move onto safer ground.

"Can you tell me anything about your husband's movements last night?"

As she carefully placed her cup and saucer back onto the tray, I noticed with some disappointment that she had not touched the tea that I had carefully prepared.

"We were planning to spend a quiet night in front of the TV with a bottle of wine. There was a film that I wanted to see. Anyway, about 7 or 7.30 Jon took a phone call."

"Do you know who from?"

"No, but he was really excited when he came off the phone. Said he had to pop out. Didn't know what time he would be back but he said that he would have a surprise for me when he did."

"You don't know where he went?"

"No, but he didn't take the car."

"Didn't you worry when he didn't come home?"

"Not really. I just assumed he had gone straight into his 'inventing' room. He spent hours in there and would often fall asleep in there as well. I just assumed he was there so I went to bed."

"And this morning?"

"When he wasn't in the workshop, I just assumed he had gone into town as usual for fresh rolls."

"Thank you." I put my notebook away and raised my head to look at her more carefully. "I know this has been difficult for you. I'll go now and leave you and Alan alone. I know that you will have things to sort out."

My reward was a shy smile that didn't quite reach her eyes. I slowly got to my feet and approached Shepherd.

"Take as long as you want, lad. If I can do anything, well …"

Shepherd raised his head and although I could see some flickers of annoyance still lurking in the corners of his eyes, I knew that we would be alright.

"Thank you, Sir." He shook my hand.

Without further delay, I turned away and minutes later I was heading down the drive and back to the station.

Fourteen

I walked into the station and beckoned Grayson to follow me as I made my way to my office. Shutting the door behind us, I sat down and removed my notebook from my jacket pocket. Grayson looked extremely uncomfortable as he stood before my desk. At six inches taller than Shepherd and twice as broad he seemed almost too big for my office space. I made a mental note – must get a bigger office.

"How's Alan, Sir?" he mumbled. For a big man he had a considerate nature and he liked to be thought of as a father figure to the younger lads. I knew that he would be feeling Shepherd's pain as if it were his own.

"He's coping. I've given him time off, as much as he needs."

"Good idea, Sir"

"Now it's down to you and me to try and make some sense of this murder. We need whoever did this behind bars and quick."

Grayson shuffled, trying to find a little more space.

"So, Grayson. Have you any ideas about motive? Neither Shepherd nor Lady Black can help me with that one. You have lived here a long time – are there any old feuds that I need to know about?"

"Nothing springs to mind, Sir. The Blacks have lived in the Manor ever since I can remember, just the two of them until Alan went to live with them as a boy. A nice couple – no enemies whatsoever."

"What about family?"

"Don't think there is anyone, Sir. They never had any

kids."

I opened my notebook and looked at the notes that I had made earlier searching for an answer.

"Well, Grayson, someone must have seen Sir Jonathon last night. He took a phone call sevenish and rushed out – never to be seen again. I want you to contact the telephone company and see if we can find out who phoned him."

"Will do, Sir."

Grayson almost skipped from the office, pleased to have something to do, pleased to feel useful. As for me – well I was left to my own thoughts. There had to be a connection to the Blacks and the wool but what? If the murderer wanted Sir Jonathon dead, why not just kill him? Why take the fleeces?

Nothing was making any sense. I needed answers and quick. Picking up my pen I chewed it thoughtfully until I was left with a bitter taste in my mouth and it wasn't just from the ink.

At four thirty there was a knock at the office door.

"Come in!"

Grayson entered waving a sheet of paper.

"Got it, Sir. There was a phone call seven thirteen last night to the Blacks from the public phone at The Cat and Fiddle."

"Brilliant! Well done!"

Grayson beamed as he left the office. The Cat and Fiddle was a public house at the furthest end of town, I'd never been in it myself as the car park always seemed to be full of motorbikes and I don't ride one. But there is always a first time for everything. I would buy myself some leathers and stop in for a drink on the way home to see what I could find out.

Fifteen

There was only one motorcycle in front of The Cat and Fiddle when I arrived. The sign was swaying silently in the late afternoon breeze and the ginger cat was grinning at me as he went to and fro, to and fro.

I stepped out of my car, crossed the yard and opened the door. Stale cigarette smoke rushed past me in a desperate attempt to escape into the open air, almost knocking me sideways. Straightening myself, I closed the door behind me and looked around. This was some place! The air was mean and the pool table looked threatening.

It was still early; the only drinker was a large guy in his forties with an enormous black beard. He was wearing a black leather waistcoat and a tattoo of an eagle was preening itself on his bulging bicep. Bet he was a real pussy cat!

My biker friend watched me all the way to the bar. I nodded to him and tapped the wooden surface. I smelt her perfume before I saw her. Her auburn hair curled over her shoulders and her green eyes smiled when she saw me. The ginger cat in person! With swaying hips, she moved slowly towards me.

"What can I get you?" she purred.

"Just a pint of bitter, please."

She pulled her lips back into a smile, revealing perfect white teeth. With feline grace she extended her arm to retrieve a tankard and proceeded to pour my pint. I watched the tawny liquid tumble into the glass and settle with a snowy white top. She placed it before me and I handed over the money.

"I've never seen you in here before, Mr Malone." How did she know my name? "To what do we owe this pleasure?" She fixed me with her green eyes.

"Just need a little help … er, Miss …?"

"Cathy Browning, but my friends call me Cat."

Now why didn't that surprise me?

"Well, Cat. I'd like to know if you remember seeing Sir Jonathon Black in here last night?"

Cat cast her eyes downwards and flicked an imaginary speck off her top.

"Last night, it was busy. I couldn't say."

"It would have been about 7.30pm."

She looked directly at me and I could see that she was nervous; she looked around her to see if anyone was watching her.

"I'm sorry, I don't remember seeing him."

"Well, if you do remember anything, you can always get me at the station." I smiled at her in what I hoped was a reassuring way. She met my gaze.

"Of course, Inspector. I will definitely call if I remember anything." With that she turned away and went to serve the silent biker.

I loosened my tie and raised the glass of beer to my lips. My throat seemed parched and the cool liquid brought immediate relief. I finished my pint and made my exit, aware that Cat's eyes were following my every move.

Sixteen

As I opened the door to my cottage, Ophelia sprang from the stairs to greet me. That was funny! Ophelia was swaying her hips in exactly the same way that Cat Browning had done earlier. I bent down to caress her face and as I lost my fingertips in Ophelia's soft white fur I found my self wondering about Cat; for all of her 'grown-up' appearance, she seemed to be just a nervous kid. Still, couldn't spend time worrying about the town's waifs and strays, I had a murder to solve. Giving Ophelia a gentle pat I made my way into the kitchen.

The beer had dampened my appetite so after filling my plate with cheese, ham and pickles and grabbing a bottle of beer from the fridge, I made my way into the lounge.

Ophelia sat with me while I ate and I fed her little slivers of ham, which she accepted gratefully. As I ate, I tried to make sense of all that was happening. So many different threads but they were certainly not knitting themselves into a nice comfortable woolly jumper. Knots and tangles everywhere. They would need a lot of unpicking.

I finished the last of my beer and settled myself down, with Ophelia in her usual position on my knee. I picked up my book and was very soon transported back to the canals of Venice where there was not a single sheep to be seen.

Seventeen

It was not even seven thirty when I walked into my office the next morning. I stared at my crime-board and felt an overwhelming urge to snap it into two. Where were the leads? I remembered the calm dignity of Lady Black. She needed closure, she needed to know why her husband had been murdered and she needed me to give her answers. But I couldn't, I had none! God, I hated this feeling of ineffectiveness.

"Sir!"

Grayson gave a gentle tap and opened the door. He entered and placed a mug of tea in front of me.

"I thought you might like this, Sir, being so early like."

"Thanks, Grayson." I took a sip and put the mug down again.

"Had any ideas, Grayson? Anything spring to mind?"

He shook his head.

"Sorry, Sir. Been thinking of it all night. There isn't a single person in this village with a grudge against the Blacks. It's a complete mystery. Did your visit to The Cat and Fiddle bring any leads?"

"Nothing! Barmaid said it was too busy and she can't say if Black was there or not."

"So, what now, Sir?"

"I want you to go to the houses opposite the pub to ask if they remember anything out of the ordinary, or even if they remember anything at all."

"Will do, Sir."

Grayson left the office and I listened as his footsteps disappeared down the corridor. Once all was quiet I opened my bottom drawer and retrieved the eyelash and the button. Placing them on my desk, I put my chin on my hands and studied them, willing them to give me answers. Blond and wearing a denim jacket. He would have stood out in this village of farmers wearing overalls and tweed jackets. Someone must have seen him. Someone must know him. Someone might even be hiding him.

The knock at the door startled me and I hurriedly replaced the evidence in the drawer.

"Yes?" I called out.

The door opened and my breath caught in my lungs as Cat Browning curled herself around the door frame. The tight skirt of last night had been replaced with jeans and today she looked even younger! Making her way over to my desk she sat down in the chair opposite me, crossing her legs. She also folded her arms across her slim body and bit her bottom lip. She seemed terrified.

"Miss Browning, Cat, what can I do for you?"

She licked her dry lips and raised her green eyes to meet mine.

"I think I may have remembered something. No, I'm sure, I do remember something."

"What have you remembered, Cat?"

"You won't tell Bob that I spoke to you, will you?"

"Bob?"

"Bob Archer, my boss. He doesn't like me talking about the customers and I need the job." I could see the beginnings of tears in her green eyes. I looked at her and tried once again to put on my reassuring smile. The tears spilled over onto her cheeks. I really needed to practise smiling in front of a mirror.

"Cat, I won't tell him."

"Thank you."

She pulled a tissue from her jeans pocket and blew her nose. A watery smile flickered across her face.

"So, what do you remember?"

"I do remember seeing someone new,' she said, keeping her eyes on her hands. "I wanted to tell you last night, but I knew that Bob would see me talking to you. He would want to know what I was talking about and would bully me until I told him. So I decided to come and see you today. Anyway, this man looked out of place, different. He was young and he seemed taller than the others at the bar, more upright and not bent over."

"Anything else?"

"I think he was blond but I could be mistaken. And I think … yes, I'm sure he was in a leather jacket. I never served him, but I remember seeing him on the phone."

"Did you happen to catch what he was saying?"

"Sorry, I was at the other end of the bar."

"Any idea when he left?"

"No. Sorry."

For the entire conversation Cat had refused to look at me.

"Cat!" She looked up. "Thank you."

So was this my guy? If so, where was the denim jacket? Or had he already disposed of it by that time? Or, was he just an innocent drinker? I took a deep breath, allowing my instinct and my logic time to retreat into a little corner of my brain and discuss the problem. A couple of moments later, my instinct stood up and announced that it was indeed was my guy. After all, from Cat's evidence, he had been in the pub and he had been on the phone. But where did that leave my investigation? In exactly the same place as before – stuck in the middle of nowhere.

She looked up and I saw that her cheeks were flushed and tears were once again brimming in her eyes. I looked at her with a fatherly concern.

"Don't worry – Bob won't find out that you have spoken to me." Her tears continued to fall and I was beginning to feel like the big, bad wolf even though I hadn't huffed and puffed once.

"Thank you," she whispered.

Looking at her as she dried her tears, I could see that she was nothing more than a very timid young girl, totally incapable of roughing it in today's harsh world; this girl needed a protector. I smiled and patted her hand. Sniffing she looked at me and once again tried to smile. Then, without warning, she leaned over and planted a kiss on my cheek.

"Thanks for being nice."

And with that she was gone. As her footsteps faded in the distance, I thought about what a sweet, vulnerable kid she was.

Eighteen

"Sir?"

Grayson was standing in the doorway, holding a brown folder which contained the lab results from the skin sample found on Felicity Spicer's hoof. Hungrily, I snatched the folder, ripping it open in my eagerness to read the findings. Surely this road was not going to turn into another dead end. I was running out of petrol.

Why were reports always boring? Why did I have to wade through inches of muddy text before finding the nugget that I needed? Page one revealed nothing of interest so turning to the second page I scanned the endless paragraphs of 'lab-speak'. Finally I found it – the sample was human skin. That was it? I threw the folder down and watched it slide off the end of the desk and onto the floor. I don't really know what I had been expecting. Past experience should have taught me that the result would have been pretty inconclusive, but all the same, a name and address would have been nice for a change.

I looked at my watch; almost lunchtime. As I looked around the office I could see that there was nothing to keep me there, certainly no leads to follow up. I needed to get out, clear my head, get a new perspective on things.

Slamming the door behind me, I marched out of the station and jumped into the car. Turning swiftly out onto the road I headed off in the direction of the local church.

The parish church of St Mary's had stood overlooking the village for hundreds of years. I had driven past it at

56

least twice a day since I had arrived here, but this was the first time that I had felt any inclination to enter it.

The heavy door creaked as I pushed it open and air thick with the scent of incense – and to my mind death - wrapped itself around me. I stood hardly daring to make a sound. Why do churches always make you want to whisper? I remembered that I had even whispered my wedding vows all those years ago. As I walked down the nave, the sound of my heels echoed all around. Sunlight was streaming through the stained glass, painting the stone floor and wooden pews in a myriad of colours. God the artist! To the right of the altar I found what I was looking for, the Lady Chapel. I sat in a pew and lowered my head allowing the silence to surround me, to calm my mind. When I raised my head again I found that eighteen minutes had passed and my spirit was calmer and stronger.

Leaving the chapel, I quickly made my way back down the nave and out into the fresh air. The light outside the church stung my eyes and I took in a huge lungful of the air of the living before returning to the station.

By five thirty all my reports had been typed. I considered phoning Shepherd to see if he needed me to do anything, or if he had had any more thoughts about the investigation, but I decided against it. In his present state of mind, he might mistake the offer as police interference, rather than an act of friendship. Picking up my jacket, I went straight home.

Nineteen

Half past eight! I should have been at the station half an hour ago! Leaping from my bed, I tried to fit a morning's routine into five minutes. Ophelia was following me around, looking for her breakfast while I was trying to put socks on with one hand and fasten my trousers with the other. I had just slapped on shaving foam and was hurriedly shaving one half of my face when I heard a knock on the door. Could this morning get any worse? Grabbing a toothbrush on my way out, I ran down the hall. Fumbling with the key, I finally got the door open just as my trousers slid to my knees.

"Morning, Sir."

Shepherd was standing on my step, his eyes widening at my state of undress. He looked paler than normal, his usual ebullience had gone, but otherwise he looked OK.

I retrieved my trousers, and my dignity, and stepped aside to let him in.

"How are you doing, lad? Excuse the mess. I forgot to set the alarm last night."

"I'm not too bad, Sir. Just need to be doing something. I can come back to work, can't I?"

"Course you can. Just give me a minute."

I returned to the bathroom and fished my razor out of the sink.

"Say, Shepherd, do me a favour and feed Ophelia, will you?" I called out. "Cat food is under the sink."

As I finished my shave, I heard Shepherd's footsteps on the hard lino of the kitchen and the opening and closing of the cupboard. By the time my face was once again as soft as a baby's bottom, Shepherd was back in the lounge with Ophelia curled up beside him, washing herself lazily without a worry in the world. Sometimes I really wished that I was a cat! He turned as I entered.

"Have there been any leads, Sir?"

"Sorry, lad, nothing concrete. Your uncle took a call from The Cat and Fiddle just before he left the house that evening. The barmaid remembers seeing a stranger - tall, young, blond and wearing a leather jacket. It could be our guy."

"Do any of the regulars remember seeing him?"

"I'm going there tonight to question them."

Shepherd nodded and reached out to stroke Ophelia who turned her head to give his fingers an affectionate rub in return.

"Well, lad, shall we go?"

Back at the station Shepherd placed himself before the crime-board, examining every detail over and over again, desperate to find some clue that we had missed. He was so engrossed that he didn't notice Grayson enter.

"Sorry to disturb you, Sir, but you need to see this."

Grayson handed me a telephone message and left. Shepherd watched as I read, noticing the darkness spread over my face.

"What is it, Sir?"

"More fleeces taken. Jim Dearing's farm. Four ewes fleeced, but this time he's killed one."

There was a sharp intake of breath as Shepherd realised that our guy had not finished yet.

"Can I come with you?"

"Are you sure you're up to it, lad?"

"Definitely. I want to catch the bas… the murderer, Sir."

"OK then, we'll pick up the camera and some plastic bags on our way out."

Twenty

Jim Dearing's farm had certainly seen better days. The barns were in need of some tender loving care and all of the farm machinery had thin coatings of rust. But for all that, Jim was the kind of man who would help any one if they were in trouble. I had even heard that he had taken a couple of his ewes over to the Spicer's farm as company for Felicity after her ordeal. Now he was the one needing help.

Jim was leaning against his tractor in the yard. As we approached he didn't even look up and I could see that he was shaking uncontrollably. He reminded me of the images that I had seen of shell-shock victims from the First World War. The horror that had met him in the field had been more than he could bear.

"Mr Dearing?"

He didn't even turn his head. I reached out and as my fingers brushed his jacket, Jim Dearing leapt into the air, his eyes wild with fright. He looked my age, but actually, he was years younger than me with a wife and baby daughter.

"Mr Dearing, it's DI Malone."

"Sorry, sorry, not thinking straight. All that blood. She was lying in it. So much blood. Why was there so much blood?"

He grabbed my sleeve and stared intently at me, trying to find the answers in my face. With a glance across to Shepherd, we both, very gently, led him back into the farmhouse.

The warmth of the farmhouse kitchen was welcoming,

but it was doing nothing to put colour in Jim's cheeks. Sitting by the fireplace he could have been an alabaster statue, he was so white. Fay, his wife fussed around, giving him a mug of tea, pulling chairs out for Shepherd and me, pouring us tea, tending the baby. She was a mini whirlwind. Finally I could stand it no longer.

"Sit down, love and tell us what you can. The baby'll be OK for a couple of minutes, and Jim, well he just needs a bit of time."

She collapsed into the wooden chair opposite me.

"Is it an awful mess out there? Jim told me to stay inside."

"Not pretty. Sorry but one of your ewes has been killed – throat cut. The other three are shocked, but OK. Did you hear or see anything?"

"Jim had gone out on the tractor earlier. The baby had just woken when I heard an engine. I just thought it was Jim, so I never bothered too much. Then I heard the ewes. I thought it was a bit odd so I picked up the baby and looked out of the window. I saw a blue van driving off."

"What did you do then?"

"I banged a saucepan."

"Sorry?" Was this a strange country ritual that I was not aware of? I looked across at Shepherd, but he was as in the dark as me.

"I banged a saucepan. It's a signal to tell Jim to come back to the farmhouse. I had an awful feeling that something was wrong and I was too frightened to go into the barn on my own."

"Blood everywhere – so much blood."

I started. I hadn't noticed Jim leave his spot by the fire and now he was standing right behind me.

"Sit down here, Mr Dearing."

Shepherd pulled a chair out for him and patted it invitingly. Jim sat on the edge, ready for flight and I focused my attention on him.

"Now, Jim, just take your time. I'd like you to tell me what happened after you heard the saucepan." I asked my question gently, not wanting to upset him any further.

"I drove over and Fay was outside. She said someone had been in the barn. She had heard the ewes bleating – they're normally pretty quiet."

"And?"

"I went in. They had all been fleeced – they were just sitting in the blood. So much blood. Minnie, Jessie and Meg were just sitting; their eyes wide open in panic, staring at Dollie. She was just laying there, blood everywhere. Then I phoned you."

"Thank you. I'm going to leave you here with your wife and we are going to the barn to see if we can find any clues as to who did this."

Jim nodded and put his head on his hands. Fay went and stood over him, putting a reassuring arm around his shoulders.

"It's a good job we sent Sallie and Lettie to the Spicers. We might have lost them too." She looked directly at me. "You will find him, won't you?"

"I will, love. That I do promise you."

Shepherd and I left them to their thoughts and walked across the yard to the barn. The guys were already in there doing their stuff, but I wanted Shepherd to cast his eyes over things. He was damn good at sniffing out clues in that particular way of his, and, he was desperate to feel useful.

Shepherd immediately dropped onto his hands and knees and set to work, ferreting away. The other guys in the team had initially been sceptical of his methods – he had been treated like a freak-show, but time and again he had proved himself, often finding that one illusive clue that they had missed. Normally they hardly gave him a second glance, but today they were watching him closely, feelings of warmth and sympathy covering the lad like a protective blanket. I also watched him; although his pain was still clearly etched into his skin, I could see that the very process of investigating this crime was in some way chasing away a little of the despair that was hanging around him – at least for a while. Leaving Shepherd thoroughly engrossed in his quest, I approached Dan Marshall, the vet. He was examining one of the sheep, his blond hair covered his face like a curtain, keeping his feelings hidden from the world. His hands, however, were gently going about their business as they examined the ewes, anxious to cause as little distress as possible.

"Dan, good to see you. What can you tell me?"

"Hi, Mike. Well, these three girls have superficial cuts caused when he was snipping the fleeces. Pretty much like the other cases. This one, however, is different. There is real viciousness here. Her throat wasn't cut when he was fleecing her – that was done afterwards.

I've no idea why – that's your job."

"Thanks."

I knelt down beside Minnie and her companions and patted their heads. Funny how I never used to like sheep, always thought they were stupid creatures who followed each other around and never had a single thought of their own. However the past few days had made me change my opinion – these were gentle, docile creatures that kept their own counsel and never harmed a living soul. They certainly didn't deserve to be violated in this way.

"Sir!"

Shepherd was beckoning me over to the doorway.

"Look here, Sir."

He pointed to a dirty area of floor. I bent down to get a closer look – at what?

"Sorry, lad, but what am I looking at?"

"Footprints. If you look closely you can make out several bloody footprints. Unfortunately some of our lads have been a bit careless; they've stepped in the blood and it has carried out of the barn with them."

Yes, I could see what the lad was pointing at, but the prints were all jumbled up.

"I think there are several different footprints here," he continued, "but I've narrowed it down to a couple that are worth taking notice of."

I listened with interest, but try as I might it still just looked like a bloody mess to me.

"I've eliminated the footprints of the team, and that just leaves these two."

With a piece of straw Shepherd pointed to a full boot print, and a toe print. The picture was becoming clearer;

I could also make out a river and a bridge. Hey, I could even see ducks!

"The full print has a thick tread, like a wellie. What was Jim Dearing wearing?"

I cast my mind back to the farmhouse and tried to picture Jim in front of the fire. Thick jacket, brown trousers and wellies. Black wellingtons.

"Black wellingtons."

"So this must be his boot print, which leaves this one. This is totally out of place. All of the others are prints of boots. Whatever type of boot or shoe this is, it has a pointed toe! Who wears pointed toes?"

"No idea, but they wouldn't be the sort of shoes to wear for wandering around a farmyard, would they? Well done, lad!"

"I hope they were expensive and that he's ruined the blasted things!" Shepherd's face was grim.

"I expect they will take some cleaning at any rate."

The team were almost finished and were just preparing to remove Dollie's body. With a nod to Shepherd we took our leave and headed back to the station.

Twenty One

He had parked his van in the lane behind The Cat and Fiddle making sure that he was off the road and obscured from view by the overgrown hedge. Now for the waiting game. It was what he did best – wait. He had been waiting for twenty seven years; he could wait another half hour.

He thought back over last night's work, and in particular, the killing of the sheep. He hadn't set out to kill it, just fleece it. He couldn't even think what it was that had made him change his mind, what had made him want to see it die. Then he remembered. It was its eyes. He was sick of seeing pleading little eyes. It had looked so pathetic that it hadn't deserved to live. What he hadn't realised was that it could be so satisfying; that it could be so energising to watch the warm blood gushing out. Such a brilliant red, and the scent! By the time he had despatched the sheep, he had achieved such a high! Sedatives and strangulation had served their purpose. Now it was time to move on. Now it was time to perhaps shed more blood, to be more inventive.

He had seen the young lad go into the pub alone. That was what he wanted – a loner. Hopefully, he would come out alone as well.

He reached into the glove compartment and removed the full syringe. Just checking. He cursed himself again for his carelessness. He would have to watch himself, couldn't allow himself to get sloppy when he was almost there. Everything had been going so well, the police wouldn't have had a clue – literally - until today. Why hadn't he worn wellingtons?

A beam of light illuminated the dark path as the door to the pub opened and then closed. Was this his target?

He ducked behind the steering wheel as voices approached. As they faded he sat up again and watched the forms of two men, one with a walking stick, disappear down the lane. He hadn't been seen.

Ten minutes later the tell tale beam of light appeared, and vanished. This time he heard no voices. This one was on his own. He crouched down and peered over the steering wheel. It was his lad. He let him walk past, let him get ten yards down the lane and then without the slightest sound he let himself out of the van, syringe at the ready.

With the grace of a stalking lioness he tailed his victim, keeping to the hedge, making sure to tread on soft grass. By increasing his stride he was soon within touching distance of his victim. He watched him as he walked. Hands in pockets, head down, in a world of his own. So easy!

With one step he was behind him. Expertly he put his right arm across the boy's mouth and with the left hand he emptied the contents of the syringe his neck. The boy had no chance to struggle, to cry out, to pray. Within one second he was on his knees, within five he was on his face on the damp track.

He turned the boy over and looked at his face. So young! His face unblemished and smooth. A mother's son. Never mind – everyone has to die sometime. No room for sentimentality. Bending down he grabbed the boy's arms and in one easy movement, he threw the still form across his shoulder. Within minutes he was back at the van.

Steadying himself against the bodywork, he opened the back door and lowered the boy inside. Pushing the legs to one side, he shut the door and returned to the driving seat. Without switching on his lights, he glided out of the lane, past the pub and set his course for the lake. Death's dark wagon taking the boy to his final resting place.

The lake was still and silent as he pulled up and got out. Stars and moon were hidden tonight. Perfect. He opened the rear door and looked at the still sleeping boy. Good-looking lad, dark hair, strong face. Bet he had a sweetheart. After all, everyone wants to be mourned, don't they?

Quickly he removed the boy's boots and threw them into the back of the van. Reaching over the boy, he located a pair of brown shoes; brown shoes with pointed toes. Once they had been very expensive and fashionable; now they were blood-stained and incriminating. Forcing the boy's feet into them, he swiftly laced them. Not a perfect fit, but no one would notice. He stood back to admire his handiwork.

With the same graceful movement as before, the boy was hoisted across his shoulders and taken the few short feet to the lake's edge. He took a few steps out into the lake and placed the boy in the water. The chill caused the boy to stir, to awaken. He smiled, he wanted to see the fear in the boy's eyes when he realised that he was going to die. With a quick movement, he pushed the boy off balance and held his face below the water. The boy's *eyes opened wide in panic, his hands grasping in vain. He watched as the boy struggled to hold his breath, he watched as the boy gulped down into his empty lungs cold water instead of cold air, he watched as the light faded from the boy's eyes. He kept holding the boy below the water for a few minutes more– just to make sure, and then, turning away, he left him floating gently into the middle of the lake.*

Stepping from the lake, he shook himself like a dog before returning to the van. Without a backward glance, he started the engine, and in darkness once again, he drove noiselessly away.

An owl in a tree hooted once as the boy slowly and gently sank from view. With a muffled fluttering of wings it swooped over the lake which was still once more, and then flew off into the distance.

Twenty Two

The next morning, Shepherd was sitting examining the crime- board again. He had already added the photos from the Dearing's farm and the whole thing was beginning to resemble a collage; a candidate for next year's Turner Prize maybe? I was definitely going to have to get a bigger board.

"I've thought of everything, Sir. There is absolutely nothing to link the farms, except that they all have sheep of course, and nothing at all links them to my uncle."

He sighed and rubbed his face. I studied him carefully, noting his lack of colour and the dark circles under his eyes. I nodded in agreement.

"We've also asked at all the farms and houses nearby. No one has seen, or knows, anyone who matches Cat Browning's description of our man. It's as if he drops out of the sky and then vanishes again like some warped superhero. I've never had such a case in all my time in the force. This chap is clever, calculating and dangerous."

"I've been thinking, Sir. Shouldn't we be protecting the farms?"

I glanced across at the board, taking in the images of the mutilated ewes.

"Well, wool still seems to be top of his list. So I think that might be a good idea. I'll get the lads to patrol the farms – will have to pay a bit of extra overtime, but if it stops another sheep being killed, it'll be worth it."

A few phone calls later and an army of police constables were making their way across the village, protectors of the sheep.

At mid-day Grayson appeared with a brown folder which he placed on my desk. Shepherd watched me as I read it, knowing that it was the result of his uncle's post mortem.

"Well, Sir?"

"High levels of sedative in your uncle's bloodstream. Chances are he was unconscious when he was killed. He wouldn't have known a thing."

Shepherd's head dropped.

"I'm glad," he whispered. "Couldn't bear to think of him struggling, and frightened."

"Funeral's tomorrow isn't it?"

"Yes, 2pm. You will be there, won't you?"

"I will, lad, but I will stay on the edge. I won't intrude."

He nodded.

"Sir!" Grayson's head appeared round the door. "Sir, Mrs Wallace would like a word. She says it's urgent."

"OK, show her in."

Shepherd vacated his chair as Moira Wallace entered. I was expecting to see the calm woman that I had seen when I had visited the farm after the attack on her five ewes. Instead I saw one very distraught woman who was struggling to control her tears. Shepherd took her arm and led her to his now empty chair.

"Mrs Wallace, Moira, what can I do for you?"

Choking sobs overcame her and she wept into her scarf, totally ignoring the box of tissues that I had put in front of her. Shepherd and I exchanged puzzled glances.

Finally she calmed down sufficiently to make herself understood.

"It's my Eddie."

"Eddie?" I looked at Shepherd who silently mouthed the word 'brother'.

"He didn't get up for milking this morning. Jim was in a right stew. Had to do it all on his own. I went to wake Eddie but his room was empty. The bed had not been slept in. I don't know where he is. He wouldn't leave without telling me. He wouldn't." She bent her head down as once again convulsing sobs overcame her.

Shepherd came over to my side of the desk and leaned towards me.

"Eddie is her kid brother, Sir," he whispered. "He's been living with them for the past 3 years. He's not the best of workers so there are always plenty of arguments between him and Jim."

I nodded and returned my attention to the sobbing woman in front of me.

"Could he have stayed with a friend?"

"No – he hasn't really made any. There aren't many lads his age around here."

"What about girlfriends?"

"He was friendly with the barmaid at The Cat and Fiddle, but it was never serious."

"Cat Browning?"

She nodded.

"What were his movements yesterday?"

"He was on the farm until 6.30ish. Then he went out, said he was going to the pub – The Cat and Fiddle. He often did after work. But he didn't come home."

She buried her head in her scarf again.

"Moira, Moira." She raised her head and looked at me through red, swollen eyes. "I want you to go home and try not to worry. He probably got drunk and crashed somewhere to sleep it off. Shepherd and I will go and have a look around and then we'll come to see you and Jim. OK?"

Moira Wallace nodded slowly and then just as slowly got up and left the office.

"Well, lad, what do you think? Could he have had an argument with Jim and decided to leave the farm? Could he have decided to head off for the city?"

Shepherd shook his head.

"No. Eddie's a bit of an idiot, but he idolises his sister and the little girl. He wouldn't run off, no matter how much Jim threw at him. Like you said, he's probably had a few too many and is under a hedge somewhere."

"Well, let's have a ride to The Cat and Fiddle anyway and see if they can tell us what time he left, who with and what sort of state he was in."

"I'm with you, Sir."

Twenty Three

Fifteen minutes later we were parking in front of the pub. As we got out and walked to the door, I wondered whether to stick to the bitter or to maybe try the mild. Shepherd turned the handle and – nothing. It was locked. Checking my watch I realised that we were too early and my stomach growled with displeasure.

"Let's wander round the back."

Through the rear windows I could see Cat tidying the bar ready for opening while Bob Archer, the landlord, was at the sink washing glasses. Archer was a short, balding man with a stomach that arrived in a room minutes before he did. He was a walking advertisement for the quality of his beer. I knocked at the window; as Bob looked up, I showed my warrant card. Cursing, he dried his hands and opened the door.

"Can we come in for a moment? I need to ask you and Cat some questions."

"Sure, if you must, but be quick about it, I've got a pub to open."

Real welcoming hospitality. Bet he was a bundle of laughs on a busy night. Shepherd and I entered and walked through to the bar with Bob Archer snapping at our heels like an overweight Jack Russell. At the sound of footsteps, Cat raised her head. Seeing me, she smiled shyly and then returned to her task.

"Cat! Get over here! The police want a word." Bob Archer was definitely a real charmer. No wonder Cat seemed frightened of him.

As Cat came around to the front of the bar, I watched

her and saw how her manner changed the closer that she got to Bob. She seemed to shrink in size, as if she was trying to hide from him. Cat saw that I was watching her and she gave a brief smile before retreating back into her shell. Poor kid! Today she looked more like a nervous schoolgirl than a barmaid. I wanted to punch Archer on the nose, but that would have to wait. Today, I had more urgent business. I took out my notebook.

"Mr Archer, Cat, I need to ask you about Moira Wallace's brother, Eddie. I believe he was here last night."

"How do I know? It was a busy night." Bob was immediately on the defensive.

"Yes, he was here." Cat looked directly at me. "Is he in trouble?"

Bob glared at her.

"No, he seems to have gone missing," I continued. "Moira is frantic. Do you know what time he left?"

"It was after nine. We had been chatting on and off all..."

"Oi, I don't pay you to chat." I was beginning to think that Archer was quite an unpleasant man.

"Please continue, Cat." I silenced him with a glare and turned back to Cat.

"We'd been chatting. He was in a good mood. He said he was going home."

"Did he leave with anyone?"

"No, he left alone."

"Did he talk to anyone else apart from you?" I felt Bob's eyes burning holes in my back.

"No."

"Is he ... er ... are you?"

"No," she gave a shy laugh, "we're just friends. We did date for a while but, well, you know."

"Was there anything strange about last night, any new faces?"

"No. Just the usual crowd."

I looked across to Shepherd to see if he had any thing to add. He shook his head, so I closed my note book and returned it to my breast pocket.

"Thank you, Cat, and you too, Mr Archer. You have been very helpful. If you do remember anything else, can you let me know?"

Bob Archer snarled and flicking his tea towel he stormed off back to the kitchen, muttering under his breath. I turned to Cat.

"Thanks again, Cat."

The shy smile returned so I just winked at her and headed towards the door. As I reached for the handle, I noticed that Shepherd wasn't behind me. Looking over my shoulder I saw him in deep conversation with Cat. Shepherd noticed me watching and, finishing his conversation, he hurried to join me. In silence, we left the pub.

Twenty Four

Grayson was rushing down the station steps as soon as we pulled up. I wound down my window as he approached.

"A body has been found in the lake, Sir."

I sighed and looked at Shepherd. This was not what we were expecting.

"It's Eddie Carter, Sir."

"Where's the body now?"

"Been taken to the morgue, Sir."

"Any signs of violence?"

"No, Sir. Looks like he killed himself, though what a young lad like him would want to do that for, I can't imagine. A real waste."

I sighed.

"Has Moira been to identify him?"

"She doesn't know yet, Sir." Grayson looked at his feet. "I was just about to go to see her."

"I'll go."

I glanced across at Shepherd but one sight of his drawn face told me that it would be better to leave him at the station. The lad had enough to worry about and enough grief of his own. He didn't need to witness Moira Wallace's distress.

"You go and write up the interview with Archer and Cat, lad. I'll handle this on my own."

"If you're sure, Sir."

"Look, when you've finished, go home. I'm sure that you and your aunt have things to sort out."

He managed a pale smile and mumbled, "Thanks, Sir,"

Getting out of the car, he followed Grayson into the station.

As I drove into the Wallace's farmyard, I considered how peaceful it was. Getting out of the car, I paused for a moment and looked around. This is what country life should be like; the sheep, their ordeal behind them, were grazing happily and the gentle lowing of cattle could be heard on the breeze. All very different to my last visit.

I knocked gently on the farmhouse door and entered. Moira had her back to me, but I could see from her posture that this was a woman who had lost hope. Nine year old Jenny was busy writing at the kitchen table.

"Hello, have you found Uncle Eddie?" Jenny looked up at me expectantly, but it was Moira that I was watching as she slowly turned to face me.

"Jenny, where's your dad?" I spoke cheerfully to the child, but kept my eyes upon her mother who was collapsing like a pile of bricks as I spoke.

"In the field. Do you want me to get him?"

"Please, Jenny."

She leapt from the chair and rushed to the door. I heard it close behind her.

"He's dead, isn't he? You've come to tell me he's dead." Moira's dark eyes refused to release their grip on mine. I stepped forward and gently taking her arm, I led her to Jenny's now vacant chair.

"I'm really sorry, Moira. I'm afraid that a body was pulled from the lake this morning. We think it could be Eddie."

She opened her mouth but her scream of pain was

silent as her face contorted in grief and finally, she freed
me from her gaze. With one swift movement she
brushed Jenny's books aside and laying her head upon
the table, she began to sob. The kitchen echoed to the
sound of her tears and I felt stranded, helpless, useless.

Moments later the door opened and Jim appeared with
Jenny in tow. One look at his wife told him all that he
needed to know. Quickly crossing the kitchen, he knelt
beside her and took her in his arms while Jenny stood
beside me, confused.

"Dad?"

Jim raised his head and looked at his daughter.

"Jenny, love. Your Uncle Eddie's died."

With a piercing wail Jenny ran over to join her
grieving parents and buried her head in her father's
shoulder. Suddenly I felt like a voyeur, an intruder
taking his pleasure as he watched a family in crisis. Not
knowing what to do, I walked over to the window and
watched the sheep grazing in blissful ignorance of the
tragedy that had befallen the family.

The sound of a chair scraping across the floor made
me turn back to the Wallaces. Jim was seated next to
Moira and was holding her hand. Jenny was sitting on
her mother's knee, her face turned away from me.

"Are you sure it's him?" Jim asked

"We're pretty sure, but we will need someone to come
and make a formal identification."

Moira raised her head and once again her dark eyes
held mine.

"You said the lake."

"Yes."

"But what was he doing there? Jim, what was he doing there?"

Jim patted her hand.

"We'll never know, love. We'll never know."

"Did someone hurt him?" Her eyes demanded an answer, but I knew that the only answer that I could give would twist the knife even deeper into her pain.

"There are no obvious signs of violence. It appears that …" Her groan stopped me from saying more.

"He wouldn't. Not Eddie. He wouldn't."

Jim moved closer to his wife and she once again sought comfort in his arms.

"I'll come along later and look at him for you," Jim said softly over the top of Moira's head. "Let me settle things here and I'll be over."

"That will be fine. And... I really am sorry."

He nodded and turned back to his family. Once again I became the intruder. Without a backward glance I left the farmhouse and made my way back to the station.

Twenty Five

It was after lunch when Jim arrived at the station. After shaking hands and offering him a coffee, which he refused, I took him over to the morgue.

"Are you OK to do this, Jim?"

He nodded but I saw his lips tighten as he struggled to contain his emotions.

I pulled open the swing doors and we entered. The room was stark white and cold. Apart from a few cabinets and a sink, it was empty – except for the table in the centre of the room; the table on which Eddie's body lay underneath a pristine white sheet.

Jim walked falteringly towards the table and stopped at its head. His fists were tightly clenched at the side of his body as he struggled to keep control. I placed my hand on his shoulder.

"Ready?"

He nodded and I slowly turned back the sheet. Immediately Jim took a couple of steps backwards, gasping for breath.

"Jim, are you OK?"

His eyes were locked on Eddie's silent face and I was surprised to see a single tear nestling on his pale cheek, like a solitary diamond on a sheet of silk.

"Jim, you OK?"

He turned his face towards me, but although he tried to speak, no words would form. He could only stare at me, helplessly.

Turning back to replace the sheet, I took my first, and my last, look at Eddie. In death he seemed peaceful, calm. What a waste! What demons had caused a lad with all of his life ahead of him to cut it short so tragically? As I continued to look down at him, I was amazed to see a hand gently brushing Eddie's hair away from his eyes. I was even more amazed to see that it was my own hand. A father's instinct to protect a child had taken over.

I replaced the sheet and turned my attention back to the living. Jim had not moved, so taking his arm I led him slowly out of the morgue and we made our way back to the station. His spirit seemed to have left him; it was like steering a robot.

With Jim seated once again before me, I phoned Grayson to ask him to bring in a cup of very sweet tea.

"Jim, I'm sorry to ask but I do need a positive ID for the file. Is that Eddie?"

"I always had a soft spot for the lad. Reminded me of me at his age. But I was hard on him. So hard on him. He died hating me, didn't he?"

Grayson's entrance with the tea stopped me from making the usual empty platitudes. Jim had been hard on Eddie, it was common knowledge. Nothing I could say would take away his feelings of guilt.

"Eddie's belongings are all sorted out for you to take home, Jim."

I reached under my desk and pulled out the paper bag containing Eddie's clothes and wallet. Jim pulled the bag over to him and opened it. As he did so his brow tightened into a frown.

"Is this some sort of joke?" Jim's sudden outburst took me by surprise.

"I'm sorry, Jim, but I don't quite understand."

Jim reached into the bag and pulled out a pair of brown shoes, a pair of brown shoes with pointed toes. I stared at them in amazement.

"These! These aren't Eddie's. Is this some sort of joke?"

As he slammed the shoes onto the desk in front of me, I could only continue to gaze at them in confusion. I had no explanation to offer him.

"Er ... the other items?"

"They're Eddie's all right, but not these," he glowered as he picked the shoes up and slammed them down on the desk for a second time.

"If you'll give me a minute, Jim, I'll go and sort this out."

Picking up the shoes, I left the office in search of Grayson. I found him at the front desk, reading the local paper. Marching up to him, the shoes were slammed down on a desk for a third time, this time by me.

"Grayson, there appears to have been a mix-up. These shoes don't belong to Eddie."

"He was wearing them, Sir."

"Are you sure?"

"Eddie is the only body in the morgue, Sir. They can't belong to anyone else."

I stared down at the boots, and a thought knocked on the door to my brain, went in and spoke loud and clear.

"Grayson, come with me."

Picking up the shoes once more, I led the way back to the morgue.

"If these aren't Eddie's, whose are they? And, why is Eddie wearing them?"

Grayson shook his head.

Approaching the body once more, I pulled back the sheet and gazed for a second time upon the boy. Again, my hand strayed to his hair, but this time with a purpose. I swept back the hair behind his ear.

"Bingo! Grayson, look at this!"

Below Eddie's right ear was a single pin-prick, exactly like the mark below Jonathon Black's ear.

"It wasn't suicide then, Sir."

"Well, it won't take Moira and Jim's pain away, but at least they will know that Eddie did not take his own life. There may be some sort of relief in that."

"The shoes, Sir? Where do they fit into this?"

Moving along the body, I revealed Eddie's feet and compared them to the shoes. The shoes were much smaller.

"Our murderer wanted to throw us off the scent. Remember the footprint that we found in Jim Dearing's barn – the one with the pointed toe? Bet it matches these."

Grayson rubbed his chin.

"So, by murdering Eddie and putting him in the shoes, he thinks that we will blame him for all of the other trouble and we will stop looking."

"Exactly! He's clever, very clever. Well, I'd better break the news to Jim."

Sitting in the office later I recalled Jim's reaction to the news that his brother-in-law had been murdered. There was the initial relief that he hadn't killed himself, but it was quickly replaced by anger that someone could

85

snuff out a life as easily as snuffing out a candle. Nevertheless, the guilt was still there in Jim's mind, guilt that he had somehow failed Eddie because he hadn't been around to protect him. As he left the office he had thanked me! Thanked me!

I looked at the shoes on my desk. A perfect size nine and a half. A perfect match for the partial print in Jim Dearing's barn. A perfect dead end for me.

Twenty Six

The gentle kneading of Ophelia's paws on my chest awakened me. I opened my eyes and looked at the clock. Ten to midnight. I must have fallen asleep. I roused myself from the comfort of the settee and groaned loudly as a painful cramp shot up my leg. Ophelia leapt from me in disgust and sat on the rug, watching me closely. After a few gentle stretches I was once again mobile and I made my way into the kitchen where my mistress was already sitting on the worktop, waiting.

"More food, Princess?"

As I tickled Ophelia under her chin, I gazed out of my window across the dark fields and sighed with contentment. The clear night sky was full of stars and a laid-back moon was watching them play benevolently while below them, the fields were laid out like a rich, velvet quilt of midnight blue. This peacefulness and calm was one of the reasons why I had chosen the country when I left the noise and grime of the city.

I was just turning back to give my full attention to Ophelia when a movement outside caught my attention. I pushed my face closer to the window, straining to make sense of what I had glimpsed. There it was again! Something was coming down the lane that passed by my cottage. It was a vehicle, a van! But the lights were off. Whoever it was who was driving, they were driving with no lights. Why?

At that moment Jenny Wallace's words came back to me.

"But I saw something, Mum. I was at the window

watching the sunrise and I saw a blue van in the lane near the sheep field. It had no lights."

This was my murderer. It had to be. There was no time to waste. Without stopping to phone for back-up, I unlocked the back door. Where were my boots? A weapon – where was my gun? Upstairs – sod it! No time! Ramming my feet into odd shoes, and grabbing a bread-knife and saucepan from the kitchen, I rushed out into the lane to do battle. Standing in the middle of the lane I raised my arms above my head, brandishing my weapons of choice. The van was getting closer. I stared hard at it trying to see the driver. Closer! He must have seen me by now! He had to stop! Stop!

Twenty Seven

As I opened my eyes a sharp pain ripped through the tissues of my brain. I shut them tightly again and groaned. I tried to raise my right hand to shield my eyes, but it wouldn't move.

"Take it easy, Sir."

Opening one eye, I saw the blurred features of Shepherd bending over me, concern evident on his face.

"Wha …? Shepherd?"

"It's OK, Sir. Grayson and I found you in the lane. We brought you back to the cottage."

"Lane? Grayson?" Nothing was making sense, but I was sure that there was something that I needed to tell Shepherd, if only I could capture that fleeting memory that was scuttling around my mind.

"You have a nasty cut on your arm, Sir. It appears that you fell on your ... er … bread-knife." Curiosity filled his voice. "Sir, what were you doing outside in odd shoes, with a knife and a saucepan?"

I could see it all now – Shepherd and Grayson bending over me in the lane, sniffing for the tell-tale scent of alcohol. They must think that I was drunk! They must think that I got drunk and went outside to … to … what? Perform an ancient pagan ritual perhaps? Or maybe it was black magic – I was preparing to sacrifice a goat and then casserole it. The tiny thought ran by me again and as I watched it, it turned around and stuck its tongue out.

"I can't remember. I remember grabbing the knife. I remember opening the door. But, I can't remember anything else. Why?"

It all sounded like a list of feeble excuses; the sort of excuses that I listen to every time I close a cell door.

"You have had a nasty bump on the head, Sir."

I tried to sit up but the searing pain once again forced my head back upon the cushions.

"Ophelia?"

"She's curled up in her basket, Sir."

I watched Shepherd carefully.

"I've not been drinking, if that's what you think!"

"Never crossed my mind, Sir," Shepherd replied with the hint of a smile playing across his face. I knew that I had to re-establish my authority and show him that I was the one in charge here.

"Why were you both in the lane anyway?"

"Another attack, Sir. Terry Hart's farm. Four ewes fleeced and his sheepdog killed. Grayson is there now. I stayed to make sure that you were OK."

"Another attack! But I organised patrols to protect the farms."

"Terry Hart told them that he didn't want protection. Told them to go somewhere else."

"The idiot! I bet he wishes that …"

I stopped as the illusive thought suddenly revealed itself.

"The van! I saw the van!"

"Sir, keep calm."

"That's why I was outside. I remember now. I saw a vehicle coming down the lane with no lights on. I remembered what Jenny Wallace had said about a blue van with no lights. I went outside to stop it."

"With a bread-knife and a saucepan?"

"There was no time to grab anything else. I had to try to stop it."

"And?"

"Nothing. I remember it heading straight for me. That's it. Next thing I know I'm staring into your baby-blue eyes."

Shepherd grinned. "Looks as if it hit you, Sir."

"Looks as if he tried to kill me, you mean. Come on, we'd better get over there."

"Are you sure you're up to it, Sir?"

"No, but I need to be there."

"Let me help you up, Sir."

Half an hour and two paracetamol later, we were standing in Terry Hart's field. Dan Marshall, the vet, was on his knees checking the four shivering ewes. Ten yards to my left a couple of old sacks covered the blood-stained body of Terry Hart's eight year-old sheepdog, Sam. I watched in silence as Dan finished his administrations and closed his bag. As he stood, his gaze strayed over to the body under the sacks and he sighed.

"Terrible business, Mike."

"The dog must have disturbed him."

"Looks that way. Throat cut, then the body kicked over there. Rib-cage was shattered, consistent with a heavy blow."

"Anything else you can tell me, Dan?"

"Nothing. Another rushed fleecing, but luckily the ewes are not too badly injured, just shaken."

"Thanks, Dan." I shook his hand and watched him leave.

Shepherd was on his hands and knees examining the ground around the sheep. Grayson had left to return to the station as soon as we had arrived.

"Anything, lad?"

Shepherd shook his head. "No, Sir."

"Look, you go and stay with your aunt. I'll finish here, and I'll see you this afternoon at the church."

Shepherd got to his feet and brushed the straw and dust off his trousers.

"If you're sure you'll be alright, Sir."

"I'll be fine, go on."

I watched Shepherd leave. His reluctance to go was understandable, after all, no one likes funerals. I remembered my father's funeral. Until he was buried it was as if he was still with me. The funeral was like closing a door, finally having to admit that he was gone forever. Some people find a sense of closure in a funeral. Not me.

Leaving the barn, I crossed the yard to Terry Hart's rundown farmhouse. His wife had died of cancer three years ago. At the age of sixty seven, Terry needed someone to help him with the running of the farm, but he was stubborn; he was determined to do it all alone. The signs of his failure to cope were all around me: the dilapidated cottage, the untidy farmyard, the rusting farm implements. Everything was slowly unravelling, slowly falling apart. I knocked and entered.

Terry Hart was sitting at the kitchen table with a glass of whisky in front of him.

"Mr Hart, it's D.I. Malone."

Terry Hart raised his head and looked at me through

92

pale watery eyes.

"Why kill my dog? I don't care about the wool, it'll grow again. But why kill Sam? It's not fair."

I pulled out a chair and sat opposite him. Close up I had a better view of the result of three years of living as a widower; the ragged shirt collar, the stained jacket. This was a man who had lost his reason for living when he had lost his wife.

"Mr Hart, did you see or hear anything at all?"

"No! Sound asleep!" He fumbled with his whisky glass and I guessed that the amber liquid was the reason why he had not heard anything. "Found poor old Sam this morning. Why kill my dog?"

Terry Hart drained his glass and reached around for the half empty bottle that was on the dresser behind him. Tears were ploughing deep furrows on his cheeks as he poured himself another glass, and drained that one too. I would give his farm another 6 months at the most before it went under.

"Thanks for your help, Mr Hart. If you remember anything at all, please ring me."

He didn't even look up as I left, his hand was already reaching out for the whisky bottle once again.

As I drove back to the station, in some pain because of my arm, I considered Terry Hart's life. First he watched his wife die, and now he was having to endure the sight of his farm slowly becoming more and more run down. This killing of his dog, a dog that I expected had been his one and only comfort in recent times, would be a devastating blow. Life had certainly stacked the odds against him.

I parked the car and went into the station. Grayson looked up from the front desk.

"Coffee, Sir? You look as if you need one. How's the arm?"

"Coffee would be good, thanks. The arm's sore, the cut looks clean enough so I think it'll heal without stitches. Anything I need to know?"

"No, Sir. No one seems to have seen anything – except you of course."

"Yes," I said through gritted teeth, "I'm the only witness. Yipee! It's only luck that I'm still here after that bastard tried to run me down."

"I'll bring your coffee in, Sir."

Twenty Eight

He sat in the van laughing. That stupid sheep-dog! Some guard dog it had been! It had trotted over to him, wagging its tail, wanting to play. A dog like that deserved to die – no bloody good to anyone. It should at least have tried to protect the sheep, barked a warning. Instead it did nothing but roll over, waiting for its stomach to be stoked. Well, he hadn't exactly stroked its stomach, he had stroked its throat, with his knife. Then, and only then, had it barked, a feeble, gurgling bark as the red blood poured out like steaming, molten ore and soaked into the field. Glorious!

As he had made his way silently down the lane, he had suddenly seen a figure rush out in front of him. That stupid policeman. He had slowed so that he could get a better view of him. The policeman had been waving a saucepan above his head, the moonlight bouncing off its copper surface. He had laughed as he had put his foot down on the accelerator. He had watched the policeman trying to decide whether to fight or fly. He had watched the policeman as he had dived to one side, trying to avoid contact with the van, and failing. He had watched the policeman as he had rolled slowly into the hedge. Then, he had driven on, in darkness.

The paperwork didn't take long. Eleven thirty. My thoughts turned to Shepherd and his aunt. How were they coping today? I had promised the lad that I would go to the funeral, but I would go primarily as a friend to lend a bit of moral support; I would also however go as a police officer to see if my guy was amongst the mourners. Would he really have the audacity to turn up today, to take pleasure in the pain that he had caused? The more crimes that he committed, the more I realised that he was capable of anything – but why? I still did not know what his motives were? I looked at the over-crowded crime-board. The only thread running through it, the only thread that was constant, seemed to be the wool. Wool! The murders of Jonathon Black and Eddie – what was the connection? My eyes fell upon the photo of the boot-print. As I remembered the face of Eddie, peaceful in death, I had the uncomfortable feeling that Eddie had just happened to be in the wrong place at the wrong time. My guy had needed to dispose of the boots. He had also needed a body – any body - to throw us off the scent. Poor Eddie!

As I stared at the board, a thought slowly unwound itself. The careful laying out of Jonathon Black's body among the fleeces suggested that not only had he been a target, but that the murderer had taken some warped pleasure in collecting the wool to be the lining of the 'coffin'. But why him? Jonathon Black was harmless! If Black had been the target, and he was now dead, why collect more wool? For what purpose? Suddenly I shivered as a black spider of realisation crawled across my skin. He was going to kill again! He was collecting more wool to be a funeral shroud for another victim! He was going to kill again!

Twenty Nine

The little stone church was almost full when I arrived.
Damn! I had intended to be there early so that I could
see the mourners arrive. Too late for that, I would have
to wait until after the service now. I squeezed myself
into a pew at the back of the church next to Len Johnson
and his wife, Elsie. Len nodded a greeting as I sat down,
and then turned his attention back to the Order of
Service. I looked around, trying to recognise people
from the backs of their heads. I could see the Spicers
sitting about three rows in front of me, deep in
conversation. Near the front I could see the red hair of
Cat Browning. Her head was bowed, in prayer perhaps,
or was she too reading through the service sheet?

Suddenly I heard the scraping of feet as one by one all
of those who had come to offer their support to Helen
Black, got to their feet. I heard the voice of the priest,
but not his words, as I watched the simple oak coffin
being carried down the short length of the nave to its
resting place at the steps of the altar. Shepherd was
supporting his aunt, his arm firmly around her. I could
not take my eyes from her. She looked even more
fragile, transparent even. Grief had taken away her
colour and all that remained was this pale copy. She
could almost have been a phantom passing by. Tears
stung the back of my eyes as I thought of her pain and
loss. I blinked them quickly away and watched Shepherd
and Helen Black take their places at the front of the
church. The service began.

The air outside had a definite sharp edge as I stood amongst the gravestones, taking a close look at the townspeople who had gathered to remember Jonathon Black. Familiar faces were gathered in small groups, talking and swapping stories about the man who was being laid to rest.

"Hello, Mr Malone." I turned and there she was, Cat Browning smiling shyly at me. "Lovely service, wasn't it?"

I nodded my agreement, and taking her arm, I led her away from the main crowd.

"Cat, can you spare me ten minutes? And, it's Mike."

"I suppose so, I'm not due at the pub until five. Why?"

"I want you to wander around the churchyard with me to see if you can spot the chap that was in The Cat and Fiddle the night Jonathon Black was murdered.

She gasped. "Oh my God! Do you think he's here?" Her hand gripped my arm.

"No, I don't really think that he would have the nerve to show up, but stranger things have happened. Don't worry, I'll be with you. Anyway, you'll be able to identify the faces that I don't know – and fill me in on the gossip."

She laughed and released my arm. "I always thought that the police had paid informers."

"I'll buy you a box of chocolates later."

Laughing again, she took my arm and we started our promenade around the gravestones.

Cat was delightful company and I did feel a pang of guilt that I should be enjoying a funeral. Nevertheless, she was very knowledgeable about the people of the town, and I would certainly be revising my opinions of some of the more solid members of the community from now on. Suddenly she stopped.

"Over there!" She pointed to a group of three people standing by the church gate.

"That's Morris and Lily Cutler from the butchers, but I don't know who the man in the overcoat is."

I followed the direction of her gaze. The Cutlers I did recognise; a large red-faced and usually jolly couple. Morris always had a rude joke or two to share over the bacon counter. The chap with them was tallish, about five feet eleven. He seemed to be late twenties and very smartly dressed apart from a very conspicuous brown fedora. I noticed with some amusement that he was wearing sunglasses! Now he certainly wasn't local! I could see his dark hair resting on his shoulders.

"Could it be their son?"

"No, Jack works in Manchester. I wouldn't have expected him to come back for the funeral."

"Could it be the guy from the other night?"

"No, he was blonde, and certainly not smart. This one is rather nice!"

"Miss Browning, really!"

She giggled and as we continued on our stroll I was reminded of another time, long ago, when I had another hand upon my arm.

"Mike, over there."

I looked to where Cat was pointing, "Who am I supposed to be looking at?"

"You see Len Johnson and his wife?" I nodded. "To

their right there is a couple I don't recognise."

The couple in question looked to be in their thirties. She was tall with long blonde hair and was dressed in jeans and a leather jacket. Very attractive! He too had longish fair hair, but he wore glasses. Like his companion, he too favoured jeans and leather.

"They don't appear to be with anyone. Are you sure that you haven't seen them before?"

"No, I'd have remembered her – she's very striking. Wait here and I'll ask around for you. It won't seem odd if I do it?"

With that she was gone. Turning back to the church gate I saw that both the Cutlers, and the mysterious stranger, had disappeared.

"The dashing young man came with the Cutlers."

I hadn't heard her footsteps behind me and I jumped at the sound of her voice.

"Seems that his name is Christopher. Len Johnson told me that he is a friend of Jack's. Apparently, he used to visit Jack regularly and he got to know the Blacks quite well."

"And the couple?"

"John McIntyre. No one knows her name. Apparently his father was a very old friend of Jon's."

"Thanks, Cat. You have definitely earned your chocolates. How would you like to be a fully paid-up police informer?"

"No thanks – I'll just take the chocolates."

"Can I give you a lift to the pub?"

She smiled. "No, it's alright thanks. I'm going home to freshen up first."

"Well, if you're sure?"

Cat reached up and kissed my cheek.

"See you around."

"Yes, bye. And Cat, thanks again for your help."

As she walked away towards the church gate I touched my cheek. She really was a sweet girl.

Thirty

He started the engine and pointing the car in the direction of the main road, left without a backward glance. He had enjoyed the funeral service; he had enjoyed knowing that he, and he alone, had put Jonathon Black's body in that coffin; he had enjoyed knowing that he was the cause of the town's grief. However, he had not enjoyed seeing that stupid policeman bumbling around with his grazed forehead. He was sure that he had dealt with him when he had hit him with the van. Never mind, if there was next time, he would do the job properly.

"Sorry, Ophelia, I'm not very good company tonight."

I stroked the top of her head and returned to my beer. The funeral had unsettled me; the look of total loss and devastation on Helen Black's face would stay with me for a very long time. And what was I doing to capture her husband's murderer? Nothing! Nothing except stumble about in the dark with a saucepan!

I pushed my beer glass to one side; I couldn't even be bothered to finish that. I had no answers. This chap was just laughing at me; he was going about his murderous business, laughing all the time at my ineptitude. I slammed my fist onto the table. Instantly Ophelia leapt off my knee and, shooting me a look of utter disgust, she retired to the lounge. I put my head in my hands and sighed.

The sharp knock at the door brought me to my senses. Upon opening it, I found a grim-faced Grayson on the doorstep. Not more bad news?

"Sir, I think you need to come to see this."

I nodded and stepped back into the hallway to retrieve my shoes and coat. Minutes later we were driving towards Terry Hart's farm.

"What's the story, Grayson?"

"When one of the neighbours popped in to check on Terry, he found the place totally smashed up and called us."

"Where's Terry Hart?"

"No idea! The neighbour didn't stay to look."

Grayson pulled up in the yard and we got out. The yard seemed still, peaceful even. I could hear the sheep gently bleating in the nearby field and the low clucking of the chickens in the hen house. Nothing else.

It was a different scene in the farmhouse, however. Chairs had been overturned, crockery smashed, books and papers pulled out of drawers and off shelves and trampled underfoot.

"Terry doesn't need this right now." Grayson's concern was heartfelt. "He's never got over Ann's death and the stupid bugger won't accept help. Who could have done this, Sir?"

I didn't answer. The memory of Terry Hart, sitting in tears with only a whisky bottle for company, swam in front of my eyes. I had a feeling that I knew exactly what had happened here.

Leaving the kitchen, I made my way upstairs with Grayson following behind. Pushing open the first door at the top of the stairs I found the bathroom. Opening the second door I found the main bedroom. I looked around in amazement; everything in here was immaculate. Make-up bottles and hair brushes were arranged on the dressing table, items of women's clothing lay neatly across the back of the bedroom chair. This was a shrine to Terry's wife. Everything was just as she must have left it. The bed however was empty. I had been so sure that Terry would have been here, sleeping off not only his whisky, but also his anger at the hand that life had dealt him.

We made out way downstairs again and out into the yard.

"Now where, Sir?"

"The field – he might be burying the dog."

Grayson switched on his torch and we made our way down to the field. As he swung the flashlight around everything seemed quiet enough; the sheep were sitting by the hedges watching us with a minimal interest. I noticed that the sacks and Sam's body were no longer there.

"Sir!"

Grayson directed the beam of light toward the far corner of the field. I could see the old tree and …

"Oh no!"

Without waiting for Grayson, I clambered over the gate and ran to the end of the field, the interest of the sheep slightly heightened by this sudden burst of activity. Terry Hart's body was hanging from the lower branch of the tree. Underneath his feet there was a patch of freshly dug earth, and a shovel. Reaching up I grasped Terry's wrist. Stone cold. He had been dead for hours. The poor fellow! The death of his dog, his only companion, had been the final straw. My murderer now had the blood of two people on his hands because in my book, he had killed Terry Hart just as he had killed Jonathon Black.

Thirty One

The next morning I arrived at the station to find a message from Shepherd letting me know that he wouldn't be in – his aunt needed him and he hoped that I would understand.

Helen Black's face materialised in my mind. Of course I understood. The woman that I saw at the funeral yesterday was not the woman that I had met a few days ago. The woman from yesterday was as fragile as a spider's web, a slight knock and she would be lost to the elements. She needed protecting until she was stronger. Shepherd had to stay with her. As far as I was concerned, he could stay with her as long as he wished.

I sat at my desk and reached for the morning's post with a grimace. My arm was still very sore. Flicking through the brown envelopes it looked as if it was just the usual boring correspondence from Head Office, after all, why send one memo when you can send twenty! I threw the bundle into my in-tray, and reached for the phone.

"Grayson, can you arrange for some flowers to be sent to Lady Black? Thanks."

Replacing the receiver, my attention was immediately caught by a white envelope that was trying to escape from the bundle of boring, brown business letters. I must have missed it earlier when I had flicked through the post and now it was waving to try to attract my attention. Picking it up I saw that it was hand-written; the capital letters seemed almost childlike in their formation. There was also no stamp, so it must have been hand delivered.

Curious! I opened it up and withdrew a small black-edged sympathy card, with the message 'Sorry to have missed you!' written in the same childish hand. A shiver ran down my spine and the memory of the van speeding towards me returned. Pushing myself out of my chair in a panic, I rushed to the front desk, clutching the card and envelope.

"Grayson, where did this come from?"

"Post, Sir," he replied without looking up.

"There's no stamp. It must have been delivered by hand."

Grayson raised his head and gave the card that I was waving in front of his face more attention.

"Oh, the white envelope! That was on the front desk when I arrived this morning."

"So you don't know who delivered it?"

"No, Sir."

"Who was on duty before you?"

"Benton."

"Contact him. See if he remembers who delivered it. Now!"

"Yes, Sir."

I left Grayson reaching for the phone and as I made my way back to my office, I was surprised to find that I was shaking. Sitting down, I took a few deep breaths to calm myself and then decided to open the rest of the letters, just in case there were any more surprises hidden deep within.

"Sir?"

Grayson appeared in the doorway.

"Sir, I contacted Benton. He spotted the envelope by

107

the door about four this morning. He has no idea how long it had been lying there. Certainly no one handed it in at the desk."

"Thanks, Grayson."

Picking up the card, I went over to the crime-board and pinned it on.

"I will catch you, my friend, and that is a promise."

Thirty Two

He could see the house quite clearly from where he had parked the van and through the windows he could see movements as the occupants passed to and fro. Now was not quite the right time. But, he had waited so long already; he could easily sit in a van for a few more hours. He had all the time in the world.

I was surprised to see that the bar was empty when I entered The Cat and Fiddle at lunchtime. Cat was engrossed in wiping down the bar and hadn't heard me arrive. I stood by the door watching her for a minute before I approached.

"Hello, Cat."

She looked up and a smile lit her face.

"Hello. Can I get you a drink?"

"No thanks, I'm just here to drop off your wages."

I pulled a large box of chocolates from behind my back and placed it on the bar before her. She giggled.

"I didn't think that you'd really buy them. Thank you."

"My pleasure."

I looked down at my hands, feeling rather like a benevolent old uncle. When I looked up again I was surprised to see that Cat was watching me, nervously biting her lip as she did so.

"I was going to call you later, Mr M... Mike." She stopped and looked around. "I finish in about ten minutes and I really need to talk to you."

"I can hang around for a while if you want."

"Please."

With that she walked over to the opposite end of the bar and carried on cleaning up. I wandered over to a corner table to sit and wait.

Twenty minutes later, Cat stood before me with her jacket on.

"So, what did you want to talk to me about?"

"Not here. Can we go back to mine?"

I nodded my agreement and as we left I was aware of Bob Archer's eyes following me.

I pulled up outside the small end of terrace cottage and Cat hopped out. Leading the way down the short, overgrown path, she unlocked the cottage door and we went in. I followed her through to her tiny kitchen where I perched myself on a stool and waited.

"Let me make you a coffee."

"I'd rather have a tea, if that's OK?"

"Tea's fine. Let's have tea."

She was fluttering around the kitchen in a state of nerves.

"Cat!"

I grabbed hold of her wrist as she passed.

"Cat! Calm down! Now, what's the problem?"

Tears were the last thing that I was expecting. I handed her my handkerchief and sat her on my stool while I finished off making the tea. At last she was composed.

"I'm sorry," she sniffed, "I expect that I am being really silly, but I think someone is watching me."

"OK, tell me – from the beginning."

"It started a few days ago. The first time when I saw a movement in the garden, I just dismissed it – thought I'd imagined it. Then the next night he was there again, there was someone standing in the garden. I did think it might have been one of the lads from the pub having a bit of a joke."

"But it wasn't?"

"No. A couple of days ago I found muddy footprints outside the kitchen window, and there were handprints on the glass, as though someone had been trying to peer in. And last night when I got home, I found this on the door-mat."

She opened her bag and handed me a photograph. It was very poor quality, but I could see that it was Cat, in her underwear, standing in front of her window.

"That's my bedroom window. You can see that I'm closing the curtains."

I handed the photograph back.

"Do you have any ideas?"

"None. None of the lads down the pub are acting differently around me. They're just normal."

I pulled up another stool and placed it in front of her. Sitting down I took hold of her hand and gently patted it.

"Cat, I'm sorry to ask this – but – could it be an old boyfriend? Have you had a relationship that has ended badly?"

"No, Eddie was the only boy that I went out with and he's …"

"Well, is there someone at the pub that has been coming on a bit too strong and is not taking 'no' for an answer?"

Her face flushed a bright crimson and I could feel the heat of her embarrassment.

"No, I'm not – you don't think – I'm not a tart. I don't

111

encourage them!"

"I never said that you were, Cat. But could you perhaps have been a bit – er – over friendly."

"No! I talk to them, I have a laugh – it's my job. And," she lowered her head, "I like being popular. Is that wrong?"

"We all like to be popular, Cat, but sometimes men can get the wrong idea."

"No! The guys at the pub aren't like that. They like me!"

"Why is being liked so important, Cat?"

"Dad left Mum and me when I was about three. He just walked out." Suddenly she reminded me of a frightened kitten. Cat needed protecting, she needed looking after, and, I was just the man for the job. I patted her hand and she continued. "Mum married again, when I was nine. I was bridesmaid. But, my step-father hated me. I was in the way and he made it clear that I wasn't wanted, that as soon as I was sixteen I had to move out."

"How old are you now, Cat?"

"Twenty two. Anyway, when I reached sixteen, I moved here to stay with a friend from school. Sally Jennings, you know, the newsagents."

"Yes, I know them."

"I stayed with them and worked in the shop to earn my keep. But again, Sally's dad didn't like me. I could tell he wanted me out too. So as soon as the job at the pub came up I left them. This cottage belongs to Bob Archer, I rent it off him."

That piece of information worried me, but I let it pass, for now.

"So?"

"Don't you see? My dad didn't like me – he couldn't have done or he wouldn't have left, would he? My step-dad couldn't wait to get rid of me. Sally's dad didn't like me being around. No one seems to like me. Am I really so awful?"

Now I could see it all. The pain of rejection going back to childhood. The loss of a father figure in her life, and a need for affection.

"Do you have any close friends, Cat? Sorry – I'm beginning to sound like an agony aunt. You can tell me to shut up if you want."

"It's OK. I feel I can talk to you." At last there was a flicker of a smile. "As I said, Eddie and I went out for a while, but we just drifted apart. Jonathon was always nice to me."

"Jonathon Black?"

"He just used to sit and talk to me when we weren't busy. He was a real gentleman. Alan's sweet too. He always wants to know if I'm OK."

"What you need is someone to take care of you. You've been coping on your own too long."

She looked up at me at last.

"If you want, I could become a sort of favourite uncle. You know, I could be around to change light bulbs, or kill spiders – that sort of thing. I could be someone for you to trust."

A smile started to break across Cat's face.

"A favourite uncle! So you'll take me to feed the ducks?"

"You know what I mean."

113

She laughed and throwing her arms around my neck, she hugged me tight. Why, oh why do I always end up looking after waifs and strays?

"Now, let's see what we can do about your night watchman."

Thirty Three

At last she was alone. As the footsteps died away, he reached into the glove compartment for the syringe. Closing the van door as silently as he could, he started to walk towards the house. At that moment he heard a car. As he stepped back into the bushes, he saw the florist's white van pass him and stop at the house. Perfect! Just what he needed. Sprinting across the gravel, he was at the back of the van just as she opened the doors to retrieve the bouquet. One blow and she was in the back of the van.

Picking up the flowers he strolled over to the house, looking around as he did so. Everything was still and quiet. He reached the door and knocked softly. The excited barking of the dogs did cause a momentary panic, but he could hear them being shut away. He heard the footsteps getting closer and closer. The door opened.

"Can I help you?"

Just some flowers, ma'am."

"Oh, thank you."

She reached out towards the flowers and immediately he let them drop to the ground as he grabbed her wrist. Before she had a chance to react, he plunged the syringe into her neck. As she crumpled to the ground, he caught her, and, sweeping her up with the bouquet, he retraced his steps and within minutes she had joined the florist in the back of the van.

Within fifteen minutes of arriving back at the station, I

had arranged for a constable to make an hourly patrol past Cat's cottage. We had talked for nearly an hour and I had the feeling that we could become good friends.

"Hello, Sir."

I looked up as Shepherd entered.

"I thought that you were looking after your aunt."

"I am. I just popped out for a few odds and ends. Thought I would see if there had been any developments."

"Not really – you heard about Terry Hart I suppose?" Shepherd nodded as he pulled out a chair. "Also, Cat Browning has a stalker. Don't think there's any connection though."

"Cat! Is she all right?"

"Yes, Uncle Mike is looking after her. I'm arranging for Morrison to add her place to his beat – keep an eye on the cottage."

"Good. Cat's OK, even if she is a bit – you know. She's a nice kid underneath."

"I know - we had a nice long chat earlier. All she needs is someone to look after her." I chose to ignore Shepherd's smile. "How's your aunt?"

"Not very good. She's not as strong as I thought she was. I hate to see her like this. I feel so – so helpless."

"It's going to take time. She'll never get over it, lad. She'll find that as time goes by the pain will become easier to deal with. It will never go away but …" I stopped. I had said too much. "Take a few days off, take care of her. If there are any developments, I'll let you know."

"Thank you, Sir."

116

I watched Shepherd leave and then removed my wallet from my jacket pocket. Opening it, I gazed at the photograph within. After gently stroking it with my fingertip, I closed it again and, with a heavy sigh, returned it to my jacket.

Thirty Four

As he gazed down at her, knife in hand, he was surprised to be overtaken by a sudden feeling of compassion. Dropping the knife, he knelt beside her. She looked so peaceful, so gentle. This was a woman who had never hurt anyone – of that he was sure. Even so, she still had to die. However, he could make her passing a gentle one. His thirst for blood had vanished as soon as he had taken in her tender beauty. Filling the syringe, he injected her again. Within minutes her breathing slowed, and then stopped. She had not felt a thing. In death she looked even more gentle.

Carefully he lowered her into the crate and covered her with the remaining fleeces. He decided that he would wait a day before he delivered her. He would get his pleasure from watching the panic that he knew her disappearance would cause.

My eyes were closed and the shadows were playing around my head. It would have been a tranquil scene, except for the turmoil in my mind. Old memories had re-awakened; it was like watching a bad film where scenes from my past were woven among the scenes of death that were now surrounding me. So much pain! Where was a romantic comedy when I needed one?

"Sir?"

I opened my eyes and saw Grayson before me.

"Sir, Shepherd is on the phone – he wants a quick word with you."

"Put him through. Shepherd, what's the problem?"

I could feel the colour draining from my face as he spoke. I put the receiver down and pushed my chair away.

"Grayson, come with me. Now!"

Within half an hour we were pulling up in front of Elderton Manor. Shepherd was at the door, waiting for us, his eyes wild with shock and terror. The Labradors were wandering around sniffing in the flower beds.

"I don't know where she is," he stammered as I got out. "She didn't say she was going anywhere, and the door was open."

I gently took hold of his arm.

"Let's go inside, lad. And, if there has been an …er…, maybe we should get the dogs inside, they might be disturbing evidence."

"Yes, of course, I didn't think."

He whistled and the dogs rushed ahead of us as I steered him into the kitchen. He shut the dogs in the utility room and sat down heavily on a stool. I motioned to Grayson to make some tea. Shepherd was in a terrible state. Fear, panic and terror covered his face.

"I shouldn't have left her. I should have stayed with her."

"Don't blame yourself. There could be a very simple explanation.

"Yes. He's taken her!"

"We don't know that. Now what time did you leave?"

"About three thirty."

"And you returned?"

"Four fifteenish."

119

"Did you see anything strange?"

"Nothing."

"You checked the house?"

Shepherd's look could have wilted a rose.

"What about the outbuildings?"

"Everywhere."

"Friends?"

"She would have left a note. Why wasn't I here?"

Grayson put two mugs of tea in front of us.

"Grayson, go back to the station. Get the lads to ask around. Did anyone see any vehicle coming to, or leaving here? I'm going to have a wander around the drive to see if I can see anything."

"No! I'll do it."

Shepherd strode out of the kitchen and opened the front door. Getting down on his hands and knees, he scanned the area around the door. He was desperate to find something, anything.

"Sir."

Straightening up, he handed me a yellow rose petal.

"Yes?"

"Look around, Sir. There are no rose bushes here."

"Could it have blown here?"

"There has been no wind to speak of for days."

"Maybe someone came with some flowers."

"There are no new flowers in the house."

As I looked at Shepherd I saw him violently flinch, as if someone had struck him with a heavy wooden mallet.

"It's him," he shouted. "He gave her the flowers and then …"

I put my arm around his shoulders.

"Keep strong, lad. You've found a clue. Well done. Maybe we can get something from it."

"How? It's a bloody petal! For God's sake it's a petal. It's hardly going to have a fingerprint on it!"

He shrugged off my arm and stormed back into the house. Anger was controlling him now. I would give him a couple of minutes.

When I entered the house again, he was sitting in the kitchen, staring out into the garden. He did not turn around as I entered.

"Alan, listen to me. We will ask around to see if anyone has bought any yellow roses in the past couple of days. We might get lucky."

"I'm sorry for shouting at you, Sir, it's just …"

"I know. You stay here in case she returns."

"No! I'm coming with you. I need to be doing something."

"If you're sure."

Two hours later Grayson, Shepherd and I were going through all of the reports that had been collected.

"A blue van was seen driving into town at about three o'clock, Sir," Grayson commented.

"A blue van was also seen leaving town about four ten, I remarked. "Do you think it's the same van? Did either of the witnesses notice the driver?"

"No one remembers, Sir." Grayson shook his head.

"What about the flowers?"

"There was only one bouquet bought today, Sir, and it was bought by … by you, Sir."

"By you!" I heard the snap in Shepherd's neck as he spun around to glare at me.

"I wanted to send your aunt some flowers – condolence. I …"

"You presented him with the perfect opportunity." There was fire in Shepherd's voice.

"No! I …"

"You gave him a perfect excuse to go to the house."

"I …"

All I could see in front of me was Helen Black's face, etched with sorrow. I had only wanted to show my respects. Now, my actions may have led to her death. I pushed my chair back and stood, hands on the desk and my head lowered. If only I could turn back time. If only I hadn't asked Grayson to order that bloody bouquet. When I raised my head, they were both looking at me in disbelief and confusion.

"Who delivered them?" I asked

Grayson flicked through his notebook.

"Janice Long, Sir. She took them."

Shepherd spun around to face Grayson.

"Janice! She'd never hurt Aunt Helen. She lives on the top road; I'll go and see her."

He rushed to the door but Grayson's words stopped him dead.

"She's not there; she's not arrived home. No one knows where she is."

"Two women missing?" I gasped. My mind could not grasp this new information. "Two women? Grayson, explain."

"Janice Long went to deliver the flowers, Sir. She was

driving the shop van – white with the shop logo on the side. She left the shop at three thirty. She never went back to the shop, she never went home. Her husband had just assumed that she was working late so he wasn't worried until we contacted him. No one seems to have seen her or the van."

Shepherd and I looked at each other.

"Aunt Helen would have recognised the van and opened the door," he said quietly.

"Would Janice have been able to overpower your aunt?"

"Never! Surely you know Janice, Sir. She's easily ten years older than my aunt. She works at the florists as a hobby."

"Grayson, did anyone see the florist's van?"

"Only when it left the shop at around three thirty, Sir."

"Right – get the lads out. House to house again! Search barns, yards, garages, everywhere."

Grayson left the office and soon I could hear him on the phone. I looked across at Shepherd who was just staring into space.

"How are you holding up, lad?"

"She's dead. I know she is."

"We don't know that. Let me run you home."

"No, I don't want to be on my own. I'll stay here … with you."

I patted his shoulder. "Alright. Come on, let's join the search."

Thirty Five

The call had come in at nine zero three. In silence, Shepherd and I drove to Weston's Garage. The young constable who was waiting for us was visibly shaken; the splashes on his jacket evidence of his vomiting.

"Are you OK, lad?" I asked him as I got out of the car.

He nodded and pointed to the area behind the garage.

"Get back to the station and we'll come and take your report later."

As he turned to go, a second car pulled up, and together we made our way behind the workshop. In the soft glow of the security light the white florist's van had an almost eerie quality. I put my arm out to stop Shepherd.

"Wait here, lad. I'll go first."

He started to protest, but then changed his mind. He stood looking at the ground with his hands in his pockets as I proceeded.

The rear door had been opened by the constable; I had to step over his vomit to reach it. I went closer and shone my flashlight into the darkness. A woman's body was lying face down on the floor of the van; she was in a pool of blood which glittered under my torchlight. I could tell instantly that it was not Helen Black. Without thinking, I breathed a sigh of relief, and then instantly I stopped my breath in horror at my reaction. This might not be Helen Black but it was still a woman who had a husband anxiously waiting for news; a woman who did not deserve this.

"It's not your aunt!" I called out to Shepherd. He came

across and together we turned the body over.

"It's Janice Long," he whispered.

Janice had been struck across the back of the head. Under the torchlight, I checked her neck for the tell-tale pin-prick and gasped. There was a pulse, very faint but still a pulse.

"She's alive! Phone for an ambulance. Good God, the constable never checked for signs of life, he just took one look and assumed."

We stayed with Janice until the ambulance arrived and then we let the team clear up. The van would be taken to the station and I would go over it for clues in the morning. My first priority was to go and call on Janice's husband and let him know the good news.

Shepherd and I returned to the car.

"Where shall I drop you, lad? You don't need to come with me to see Janice's husband."

"Aunt Helen's. I've the dogs to take care of, but, I don't want to be on my own. Sounds silly at my age, doesn't it?"

"Not at all, lad. Do you want me to come back and stay with you?"

"Would you, Sir?"

"Of course. I'll just have to sort Ophelia out. Can't bring her, she doesn't like dogs."

"Thank you, Sir."

A thought occurred to me and I realised that I had the perfect solution to both of my 'cat' problems.

Thirty Six

The interview with Ben Long had been very quick and I had driven him to the hospital to be with his wife. She was still unconscious but the signs were good. Good for me too. At last I had a witness who might be able to give me the vital clues that I so desperately needed.

I stopped the car outside Cat Browning's and knocked on her door. No reply! I glanced at my watch. Damn! Ten forty three! She would still be at the pub. Getting back into the car, I drove the few hundred yards to The Cat and Fiddle.

Cat's face lit up when she saw me at the door. I looked around; it was a relatively quiet night. There was a group of lads playing darts; an older group were sitting at one of the tables and there were two chaps at the bar.

"Hello!"

"Hi, Cat. I need to talk to you. Do you have a moment?"

"Sure."

We went down to the opposite end of the bar where we would be able to talk in privacy. I could see Bob Archer glowering at me, but I just smiled at him and then turned my back.

"Cat, I want you to keep what I am going to tell you to yourself. You mustn't breathe a word. Do you understand? I can trust you, can't I?"

"Of course."

"Helen Black is missing. It looks as if … well, we're thinking the worse."

"Oh my God." Tears sprang into her eyes and she gripped my hand. "Not her, too? Poor Alan! How is he?"

"Not very good. That's sort of why I'm here. I need to ask you a favour."

"Anything."

"Alan doesn't want to be on his own, I'm going to stay with him. But, I need someone to look after my cat. How do you fancy a bit of house-sitting?"

"I'd love to. Anything to help. It'll get me away from my night watchman as well. I might even be able to get a good night's sleep."

"Would Bob mind if I took you away now?"

"Probably."

"Good!" I was going to enjoy this.

Bob Archer was still watching me like a hawk as I approached him.

"Bob! I need Cat to come down to the station with me now. You don't mind do you?"

He looked straight through me as if I wasn't there.

"I'll knock an hour off your wages."

"You do that," Cat retorted.

She disappeared into the back and seconds later had returned with her jacket and bag. With a glance at Bob, who now had a face like thunder, we left.

By ten past eleven Cat was safely installed in my cottage, and I was on my way back to Elderton Manor. In the beginning, Ophelia hadn't approved of a second 'Cat' in the cottage; she had glared at her through glittering green eyes and had wandered off to sit in my chair with her back to us. However, a few tit-bits later and she was sitting on Cat's knee, purring contentedly, and preparing for a girlie night in. The only things missing were a chick-flick, a box of tissues and popcorn.

All the lights were on in Elderton Manor when I arrived and I could hear the dogs barking to announce my arrival. As I switched off the engine, Shepherd appeared at the door. In the short time that I had been away he seemed to have aged ten years. He shut the door behind me.

"Any news?"

I shook my head. "I popped in at the station on my back, but nothing. Sorry. You need to get some rest, lad."

"I can't sleep - not knowing she is lying dead out there."

"We don't know that."

"I do! I do! Why her? She is – was – so gentle and kind."

"Don't give up hope, lad. Everyone is looking for her, we might be lucky." I led the way into the lounge. "Lay down here and I'll fetch some blankets. Er … where are they?"

"Upstairs – airing cupboard."

"We'll both sleep in here tonight."

As I left the lounge I turned to look back at Shepherd. His white face was staring into the fireplace while his hands were twisting a scarf that I guessed belonged to Helen Black. With a heavy sigh, I went to get the blankets.

The clock striking three woke me and I stretched. My

neck was stiff after a couple of hours sleeping in a chair. I looked across at the settee where Shepherd had finally fallen asleep just after one. In sleep he was so young and vulnerable. The father in me wanted to comfort and protect him; the police officer in me knew that there were boundaries that should not be crossed.

Thirty Seven

"Tea, Sir?"

I opened my eyes and Shepherd was standing in front of me with a mug of steaming tea in his hand.

"Morning, lad." I looked at my watch. Six forty five. "Thanks. How are you bearing up?"

"You know."

He handed me my tea, then went back to the settee. His blankets were neatly folded, and looking at him again, I could see that he had already showered and changed.

"Did you get much sleep?" I asked him.

"More than I thought I would. So, what do we do today?"

"Check how the search is going. You and me can check over the florist's van and see if there are any clues. Also, check for more sightings of the blue van. We won't give up looking."

He nodded, and watched me as I sipped my tea.

"Have you eaten, lad?"

"Couldn't face it."

"You need to … sorry, I sound like my mother. I'll shut up."

Shepherd said nothing.

The sudden barking of the dogs surprised us both. Then we heard the knock on the door. Shepherd got up to answer it and I followed closely behind. John Bellamy, the milkman was standing on the doorstep.

"Morning, Al. Just five pounds twenty five, please."

"Oh, yes, of course." Shepherd fumbled in his pocket

and pulled out several coins, which he counted out and handed to the milkman.

"See you next week, Al."

John turned back to his van and I followed him.

"Are you usually around the town at this time every morning?"

"I'm usually earlier than this, but today's the day I collect the money. Always takes longer as folk like to chat."

"Have you ever seen a dark blue van around? It might even have been driving with its lights off."

"No – don't recall. Hang on – yes! There was a chap driving with his lights off the other morning – stupid bugger – near your place, guv."

"Did you get a look at the driver?"

"Youngish, I think. Could only see an outline when I flashed him. Think he had long hair, though it might have been a girl. But maybe not, what sort of girl goes driving around at that time in the morning?"

"Did you notice which direction he went in?"

"Left at the bottom of the lane, heading out of town."

"Thanks a lot."

Shepherd was in the kitchen washing up the mugs; he had already placed the blankets at the bottom of the stairs ready to return to the airing cupboard. As he was wearing his boots and jacket, I took the hint.

"OK, shall we go?"

He dried his hands, and we set off for the station.

Grayson was still on duty when we arrived.

"Morning, Sir. Alan."

"Morning. John Bellamy, the milkman, saw the van that hit me heading out of town. Can you arrange to follow that up and see if anyone else saw the van heading in that direction? Try asking in the next village as well. Let's widen our area of enquiry."

"Will do, Sir. The florist's van is in the second garage. I have reports of it being seen driving up to Elderton Manor at about quarter to four and leaving again about five minutes later."

"Good. Did anyone see the van being driven into Weston's Garage?"

"No one has come forward yet, Sir."

"OK. Anything else?"

Grayson flicked through the sheets in front of him.

"Yes. Morrison chased a chap at Cat Browning's last night. Spotted him leaving the garden, so he ran after him. Unfortunately, Morrison lost him."

"Description?"

Young, blonde hair, jeans and leather jacket."

"Did Morrison recognise him?"

"No, Sir."

"OK. Thanks."

Shepherd and I made our way out into the yard. The report of the intruder at Cat's worried me. I was glad that I had moved her out of her cottage. At least I knew she was safe.

The florist's van had been parked at the back of the garage. Looking at it standing there no one would guess its guilty secret. I opened the rear doors and saw that the pool of blood had congealed overnight. Putting on our protective gloves, Shepherd and I started to make a closer inspection of the interior. I tried not to be unsettled by the very clear outline of Janice's body in the blood.

"Sir!"

Shepherd held up some blood-stained fibres."

"Wool?"

"No, Sir. It looks like thread from my aunt's shawl."

I straightened.

"Are you sure?"

"Yes – I think so."

"Looking at the floor of the van, there is no evidence that a second person was in here. There is only one clear outline," I said gently. Shepherd was still staring at the fibres in his hand.

"Nevertheless, still bag them."

I continued searching while Shepherd went off to get some evidence bags. Suddenly, I spotted it, but I could not make sense of it.

"Janice Long," I called to Shepherd, "what colour is her hair?"

"Greying, Sir." Shepherd returned to my side and I turned to him, holding up a long blood-stained hair.

"Can you make out the colour?" I asked.

"Not really, Sir. It looks dark, but that could just be the dried blood. It could just as easily be blonde."

"Look at the length. It must be at least waist length, too long for Janice. What is it doing in the blood? Could he have an accomplice?"

Shepherd shook his head.

"There has been nothing else to suggest a second

person being involved."

"Maybe he didn't need one until now. He knew that your aunt would not answer the door to a man."

Shepherd was struggling to follow my reasoning.

"But there is no evidence of two people. Even the milkman only saw one driver."

"She might have been in the back. If she was local she would stay out of sight or someone would recognise her."

Shepherd just shook his head. "I'll bag it, Sir."

He was not convinced and to be honest, neither was I, but, at that moment I could think of no other explanation for a long hair being part of the crime scene.

By lunchtime we had the reports on the evidence found at the van. The fibres were consistent with being from a lady's shawl, and the colours matched those of a shawl that belonged to Helen Black, but was missing. The hair was blonde. Unfortunately the evidence confused us rather than helped us. Who was the mystery blonde?

"Nothing is making any sense, Sir."

"I know."

Shepherd sighed. "The chap at Cat Browning's – is it possible that he is connected to all of this?"

"I honestly have no idea. The answers to this case seem to be getting further and further away from us. If he is connected with the case – what is the connection between Cat and your aunt and uncle?"

"As far as I know there is none."

"Exactly – nothing makes sense."

"Sir," Shepherd looked at his watch. "I really need to

pop back and feed the dogs."

"I'll drive you."

Thirty Eight

Shepherd saw the crate by the front door before I did. His anguished cry tore at my heart. I spun the car around.

"Stop! Stop! I've got to go to her."

I ignored him and putting on the siren, I sped back to the station. Stopping the car, I turned and gripped him by the shoulders. He was fighting me to escape.

"Listen! Alan! Listen to me! We have to do this properly, carefully. I know it is hard, but we cannot go rushing in and destroying evidence. Do you understand? Do you understand?"

He stopped struggling and looked directly at me through eyes that were swimming with tears. He nodded.

"Good lad. Wait here while I get the team to return with us."

Leaping out of the car, I ran into the station and within minutes we were leading a convoy back to Elderton Manor.

I held onto Shepherd's arm as the lid to the crate was prised off. Already I could see that this was a twin to the crate in which Jonathan Black had been found. Wool was once again pushing through the wooden slats, trying to escape from the horror within.

Carefully, the first fleece was lifted, and just as carefully placed on the plastic sheeting that had been spread around the crate. As the team made to lift the second fleece, I could feel Shepherd holding his breath. I found that I was doing the same.

136

"Sir!"

I stepped slowly forward. My arm was around Shepherd's shoulder and I was gripping him tightly. His breath escaped in a sob as he looked down into the crate at Helen Black. She was cushioned within the remaining fleeces and looked so peaceful. You could almost imagine that she was sleeping, if it were not for the greyness of her skin. Shepherd wrenched himself from my grasp and leaned into the crate. Very gently he lifted his aunt and clasped her to his breast as tears spilled from his eyes. Slowly, I approached him and touched his shoulder.

"You're damaging evidence, lad. Let her be."

He shrugged me away and held her even tighter.

"Alan!"

Finally, he released her and carefully laid her back within her makeshift coffin. Looking down at her face, gentle even in death, I cursed the person who had done this. There were no visible signs of violence, no tell-tale bruises on her throat, and I thanked God silently for this. I leaned over and gently brushed her hair aside. Two pin-pricks. Hopefully the injections had killed her outright. I would have hated for her to have felt fear or pain. I stood and took a firm hold of Shepherd once again.

"Come on inside, lad."

I steered him into the house and closed the door behind us. I didn't want Shepherd to watch as the team completed their duties.

I handed Shepherd a cup of hot sweet tea. He was sitting at the kitchen table with his head in his hands.

The sun shining through the kitchen window seemed to miss him completely, leaving him alone with his grief.

"Here, drink this."

"I don't really …" He didn't even look up.

"Come on, it'll do you good. Now, are you going to be OK on your own?"

"Aunt Helen and Uncle Jon were the only family I had. Now there's no one."

"Look, do you want me to stay here for a bit longer?"

He looked up for the first time.

"I don't want to be on my own. Are you sure, Sir? I don't want to be … you know."

I sighed.

"No trouble at all. I'll just have to check that Cat is happy to stay with Ophelia."

"Thank you, Sir." He picked up his mug again and lapsed back into silence.

Back at the station later, I went through the reports. Helen Black appeared to have died as a result of the injections. As I had expected there were no clues on the crate and no one had seen any vehicle driving to or from Elderton Manor. My only hope now lay with Janice Long, when and if she regained consciousness. For safety's sake, a constable was staying with her at the hospital. The blonde hair remained a mystery.

"Grayson!" The familiar shape appeared in my doorway. "Can you check with the witnesses who saw the florist's van if they can recall the driver?"

"Certainly, Sir." He disappeared as quickly as he had arrived.

138

Cat Browning's stalker – there was something about the constable's description that was jabbing me sharply in the back. Fair hair, jeans, leather jacket. Why did that seem familiar?

Pushing myself out of my chair, I moved over to examine the ever more crowded crime-board. The jabs in my back increased in intensity as my eye flitted over all the various pictures and transcripts. Got it! The description almost matched Cat's description of the guy that had been in the pub the night that Jonathon Black disappeared. Blonde hair and a leather jacket. Coincidence? I didn't believe in coincidences. But, if this was the same guy, what had Cat Browning to do with all of this? Was she on his list? I didn't like it – not one bit. I needed some air.

Fifteen minutes later, I was heading up to my own front door. I knocked and entered.

"Cat. It's me, Mike."

She bounded from the kitchen.

"Hi, I was just making a coffee and a bite to eat, do you fancy one?"

"That'd be great."

As I walked into the kitchen, I spotted Ophelia curled up on the kitchen chair. She opened one eye and gazed at me.

"Hello, Princess. Have you missed me?"

She raised her head and yawned slowly. Then having stretched herself elegantly, she stepped down from the chair and wound herself around my legs. I reached down and picked her up. Immediately her damp nose nuzzled my neck. It was nice to be back home, even if it was just for a cup of coffee.

"She's a real sweetie," Cat said over her shoulder as she poured the boiling water into a second mug. "She came and slept on the bottom of the bed last night.

"That shows that she's accepted you into her house."

I took my sandwich and mug and followed Cat into the lounge.

Sitting down I took a deep breath.

"Cat, we found Helen Black's body a couple of hours ago."

"Oh, no! Poor Alan! Is he OK?"

"No – not at all. He was sleeping when I left him. Look, I'm going to need to stay with him a bit longer – help him to sort things out. I was wondering if you were able to stay here until …"

"Of course! No problem – anything to help."

I reached for my wallet.

"Look, here's twenty five pounds for food and stuff. I never keep a lot of food in the house, except for cat food of course."

She took the money and grinned. "And now I'm going to need 'cat' food too. Does Alan need anything?"

"Friends and support. He said that he has no one close."

"He's everyone's mate, but not their friend, if you know what I mean." I nodded. "He always seems to be part of a group. As friends go, I suppose he talks to me more than anyone."

"Then he's going to need you, Cat."

"I'll pop and see him later."

I took a bite of my sandwich to give me the courage to raise my second subject.

"Cat, your stalker returned last night. Unfortunately the constable wasn't quick enough to catch him."

"Who is it?"

"He didn't get a good look at him. It's good that he still thinks you are at your cottage though. If you give me your keys, I'll arrange to leave some lights on so that he keeps thinking that you are at home."

"OK."

We continued eating in silence. I had been going to tell her who I thought her stalker might be, but had changed my mind. I didn't want to scare her. I decided to let her think that I had everything under control.

Shepherd was still asleep on the couch when I returned. I put my overnight bag down in the hall and went to the kitchen to make him a bite to eat. He appeared in the doorway just as I was breaking eggs into a pan.

"I could smell the oil."

"How are you feeling?"

"Like it's all an awful nightmare."

He sat at the kitchen table and watched me as I fried the eggs, listening to the popping sound of the oil.

"Have you got any more details, Sir?"

"Well, Cat is happy to stay at my cottage for as long as I need."

"I didn't mean that."

"I know. Let me finish this and then we can talk properly."

I put the egg and bacon down in front of him and watched him as he pushed it around the plate.

"Try and eat something, lad."

"I … is there any news?" Anguish was etched on his face.

"The florist's van was seen being driven by Janice Long on its way here. However, when it was spotted later a woman with blonde hair was driving it."

"A woman! A woman killed my aunt?"

"I don't know. Maybe this woman was an accomplice. She drove the florist's van away and our guy stayed to …"

"To kill her."

"We need to speak to Janice Long. She may be able to fit some of these pieces together."

Shepherd picked up a forkful of bacon and began to chew slowly.

"There is another thing, lad."

He put his fork down and waited.

"Cat Browning's stalker. From the description it could be the chap that was in The Cat and Fiddle the night your uncle disappeared."

"What?"

"I know. Nothing makes any sense. If this is the same guy, why the interest in Cat?"

"Is she safe?"

"I've been to her cottage and switched on some lights to make him think she's still there."

"If I were you. I'd get someone to watch your place too, Sir. Just in case."

I nodded. "I think I will."

As I watched Shepherd slowly chewing his food, I thought of Cat alone in my cottage and rewound the events of the past few days. What had I actually achieved? Nothing except an ever-growing pile of the dead and the suffering. Was I destined to be always hounded by Death? I had left the city to escape him, but now it seemed as if his grasp on me was even tighter.

Thirty Nine

The phone woke me at eleven thirty. I had been in bed less than an hour.

"Malone."

"It's Grayson, Sir. Some more sheep have been attacked."

"What! Where?"

"Outside town, Sir. The Henson's farm, two miles to the west."

"The patrols?"

"They were only covering the nearby farms, Sir. Not enough manpower for more."

"Damn! I'll be right there."

As I opened the bedroom door, Shepherd was standing on the landing."

"I heard the phone, Sir."

"Another sheep attack. The Henson's place, do you know them?"

"Yes. I'll be ready in five minutes."

"No, you stay here."

"And do what? I'm better off being busy."

"OK. To be honest, I'll be glad of the company, and a guide."

Dan Marshall was already there when we arrived. He got to his feet when he saw Shepherd and came across to offer his condolences. I went over to look at the two sheep that were sitting shivering in the corner of the field. Immediately I noticed that care had been taken to remove their fleeces; the sheep had not been injured. Our chap's blood lust seemed to have abated – for the moment. He had evidently felt safe from interruptions here. The farmhouse was some way from the field, and there were no nearby lanes; there would be no passing traffic to observe him at work. Part of me was pleased that the sheep were unharmed. But, part of me was now very afraid. If he was collecting more fleeces. It could only mean one thing. He had another victim in his sights.

An hour later and we were on our way back to Elderton Manor. All the photos that we needed had been taken, and Shepherd had scanned the ground. No clues. George Henson and his wife had heard nothing. I hadn't expected them to have done really, judging by how far away they were from the field.

"I'll start the paperwork in the morning. Let's get you home, lad. You look done in."

Shepherd did look exhausted. The past few hours had taken their toll. So, by two o'clock we were both tucked up in our respective beds. Unluckily for me, sleep was far away. The thought that another victim was being targeted was too dreadful to contemplate. This guy was in the fast lane, and I was barely treading water. I felt totally out of my depth and while I was struggling for answers, people were dying.

Forty

"Sir! Sir!"

Shepherd's gentle shaking woke me. I looked at the clock. Six thirty! I must have dropped off after all. He handed me a mug of tea.

"Sir, will you come with me to sort the funeral out? I don't know who else to ask."

I nodded as I drank.

"Ring them and arrange for us to go at lunchtime. What are you planning to do today?"

"I thought I'd come into work. I just don't feel like staying here on my own."

"Well, if you're sure. And tonight if you are feeling strong enough, we could make a start sorting things out here. After all two pairs of hands are better than one."

He nodded his agreement.

"And … er … have you had any thoughts about what you will do with the house?"

"No, although I would like to keep it. All of my happiest memories are woven into its fabric. Not sure if I could afford to run it however," he looked slyly at me, "unless of course there's a pay-rise going."

"You need to speak to the PM about that one, lad. In fact we all do. This government undervalues our profession, but don't get me started on politics this early in the morning."

"Seriously, Sir, I would like to keep the house if at all possible. I'd hate to see someone else living here and tearing things apart. And I certainly have no room for the dogs in my cottage."

"You could always take in lodgers. There's plenty of room."

"Maybe," but the grimace on his face told me that he didn't want strangers trampling over his aunt and uncle's possessions. He got up and made for the door, "Breakfast in half an hour, Sir. I'm starving so I'm doing the works. Is that OK for you?"

"Sounds fantastic."

I watched him leave. He had suffered terribly in the last few days, but he would pull through. Touches of the old Shepherd were already beginning to peep around the corners of his aura. He would be fine.

Grayson was just going off duty when we arrived at the station.

"Morning, Sir. Alan."

"Morning, Grayson. Anything I need to know about?"

"No reports of any vehicles near the Henson's farm, Sir. And the hospital phoned. Janice has regained consciousness. That young constable is staying close to her like you asked."

"Thanks." I turned to Shepherd. "Are you up to going to see her?"

"I'll be fine, Sir"

Shepherd was out the station and back in the car before I had chance to say another word.

Forty One

"I don't want you tiring her."

The Sister stood barring the way to Janice Long's room and I could feel myself shrinking under her stern gaze. Me! Afraid of a hospital sister!

"We only need to ask her a few questions, Sister. Ten minutes at the most."

"I'll be timing you."

She marched back to her desk and after tapping at the door, Shepherd and I entered. Janice was sitting up in bed with her head heavily bandaged; her husband was sitting beside her, grasping her hand tightly. She looked up and greeted me with a smile. However, as soon as she caught sight of Shepherd behind me, her smile faded and her eyes filled with tears.

"I am so sorry. Your aunt was a lovely, lovely lady. I'm so sorry. It's my fault. If only I had fought back – if I had …"

"No! No." Shepherd took her hand in both of his and sat on the bed beside her, looking closely at her. "It was not your fault. Don't ever blame yourself. This person is evil, pure evil. Be thankful that you escaped with your life, but don't ever, ever blame yourself for Aunt Helen's death."

"She was so sweet and kind. It's not fair."

"That's why we need to catch him. We need to stop him doing it again."

I stood watching Shepherd with admiration, the way that he was comforting Janice, even in his own darkest moments. I took a step back to allow him to carry on talking to her.

"Mrs Long, Janice, we must catch him. Can you remember anything at all about what happened? Anything, no matter how small and silly it might seem – it might be just the clue we need."

She freed her hand from her husband's tight embrace and patted Shepherd's hands. She took a deep breath before continuing.

"I parked outside the house. Everything was quiet and I never saw anyone in the lane. I got out and went to the back of the van to take out the bouquet. I opened the van doors and then I heard footsteps. As I started to turn, she hit me."

"She?"

"All I saw was long blonde hair, but she was tall and very well built. Didn't see her face, just the hair."

Shepherd caught my eye and I nodded. He turned back to Janice.

"Can you think of anything else? Noises? Smells?"

"Only my husband's aftershave."

"I'm sorry."

"When I was hit, I thought I could smell George's Dunhill aftershave. I know it sounds daft, but I felt as if he was with me somehow."

She turned and took hold of her husband's hand, her eyes gleaming.

"Thank you, Janice. You've been a great help."

Shepherd patted her hand and stood. After making our farewells, we left.

"A woman?" Shepherd queried as soon as we were in the corridor. "A woman wouldn't be doing this."

"Nothing makes sense," I agreed. "But, we know a woman was at your aunt's. We know a woman hit Janice Long and drove the van away from the Manor. However, I agree with you. Carrying drugged bodies, manoeuvring crates – that needs strength."

We left the hospital and headed for the car. As we walked, I sniffed the air to rid myself of the scent of disinfectant and a thought occurred to me.

"Hugo Boss?" I asked Shepherd.

"What, Sir?"

"You're wearing Hugo Boss. I can smell your aftershave, lad. Janice said that she could smell her husband's aftershave."

We reached the car and got in. I started the engine, but made no attempt to move.

"She said that she could smell his aftershave. Why? The mind playing tricks on a woman who believed that she was going to die – giving her comfort in her hour of need perhaps?"

Shepherd didn't answer; I could see his mind working. "It could be, Sir."

"Or, what if it was her attacker's aftershave?"

"A woman wearing aftershave? So who are we looking for now – the bearded lady?" He was angry at what he perceived to be my foolishness.

"Calm down, lad, and listen. Janice said that her attacker was tall and well-built. What if it wasn't a woman at all but a man wearing a blonde wig?"

"A wig?" His mood was certainly not improving.

"Would your aunt have opened the door to a strange man?"

He shook his head and I could see that gradually he was beginning to follow where I was leading.

"But, if when she looked through the glass she saw a woman with long blonde hair – well, she wouldn't be afraid, would she? She would open the door."

"And this woman would be holding flowers."

"Exactly. A blonde wig was used to deceive your aunt – to get her to open the door."

"And Janice?"

"Another Eddie – in the wrong place at the wrong time – only she was lucky, she survived."

"He must have thought that he had hit the jackpot when Janice's van pulled up." Shepherd sighed. "A perfect excuse to get Aunt Helen to open the door."

"At the moment he seems to have luck on his side, but it will run out soon."

Shepherd fastened his seat-belt. "I hope so, Sir."

Forty Two

I dropped Shepherd at the house and drove to The Cat and Fiddle. The meeting at the undertaker's had been difficult for him, I was glad that he had asked me to go along; he would not have been able to cope on his own. Now, he wanted to be on his own, and I respected that.

However, I now had problem number three to sort out. When I had arrived at the station there was a message waiting for me. Cat had phoned the station asking to speak to me urgently – could I go to the pub to see her? I had an awful feeling that I already knew what her problem was. Morrison had informed me that there had been no sign of the stalker at Cat's cottage last night – did that mean that he had found her again? I would call in at the pub on my way home.

I could tell from her body language as I entered that she had been watching the door ever since opening time. Relief spread over her face as soon as she saw me. As usual Bob Archer was standing at the corner of the bar, glaring at me. Animosity seeped through every pore on his body. How I would love to find something on him. One day!

"I'm so glad to see you. I phoned the station, but they said you were out." Her cheeks were pink with agitation,

"Don't worry, I'm here now."

"He's found me!" My heart fell into my boots. It was just what I had feared.

"Tell me."

"Ophelia really lost it last night. She jumped off the

152

bed and onto the window-sill. Her fur was on end and she was growling. I thought it was another cat, but when I got out of bed to have a look, I saw him. He was staring up at the window. How did he find me?"

"Did you tell anyone where you were staying?"

"No, of course not." Tears filled her eyes.

"Did you get a good look at him?"

She sniffed. "Tall, longish hair, jeans, leather jacket."

I took her hand. "Cat, do you think it was the guy that was in here the night Jonathon Black disappeared?"

Immediately, I regretted asking the question. Horror caused the colour to fall from her face. She stumbled forwards and grabbed my arms.

"No! It couldn't be him, could it?"

"You saw him, Cat. Do you think it was the same person?"

"I don't know. But what would he want with me?" She sniffed again.

"I don't know, Cat. I don't know."

As her tears began to fall, I leaned over the bar to comfort her. Bob Archer's face was a picture of pure fury.

I had decided to wait at the pub until closing time. Cat had got herself into a real state and I didn't want to leave her alone with the 'understanding' Mr Archer. As he was locking the door she came over to me, coat on and ready to leave. She was still very pale; I needed to catch her stalker and put her mind at rest. We left The Cat and Fiddle under Bob's watchful, malevolent gaze and the journey back to Elderton Manor was made in silence. I

153

had phoned Shepherd and we had decided that it would be better for Cat to stay at the Manor with him. I was beginning to feel like a mother hen gathering my brood around me.

Pulling up outside the house, I opened the door for her and together we went in. The Labradors rushed towards us, eager to welcome yet another person into their home. As they pushed their noses into her open palms to welcome her, she knelt to pat them both and they responded with beating tails and slobbery kisses. Shepherd appeared at the door of the lounge. Catching sight of him, Cat got to her feet and went across to hug him.

"Oh, Alan. How are you?"

After half an hour I made my excuses and left, but not without checking that everything was secure. I even wandered around the garden with a flash-light. As I pulled out of the drive, I saw the patrol car that I had arranged to be stationed at the end of the lane. I was not taking any chances at all.

Pulling up at my own cottage and opening the front door again felt so good. Ophelia was sitting at the kitchen door, purring loudly as I kicked off my shoes, pleased to have me home.

"So, you missed me then, did you, Princess?"

She had jumped onto my knee before my bottom hit the chair, quickly settling herself so that she could gently knead my chest, calming me. However the fear that his next victim might be Cat Browning was disturbing. If only I could find the link between her and the Blacks; if

154

only I could discover his motive, then I might just be able to catch him.

Forty Three

He watched the policeman drive away in his green car with some pleasure.

"It is so kind of you," he whispered, "to make things so easy."

The next morning I arrived at the station in a sombre mood. Shepherd hadn't arrived but to be honest, I wasn't really expecting him to be in. However, just in case he did arrive, I closed my office door. I didn't need him, or anyone, to know about this phone call. Flicking through the phone book, I soon located the number and dialled.

"Simon, it's Mike Malone. Hope it's not too early?"

"Good to speak to you, Mike. No it's fine; my first client isn't due until quarter past. What can I do?"

"I need to ask you something off the record, Simon. It's about the Blacks. I understand that you are the family solicitor?"

"Yes."

"I wouldn't normally be asking, Simon, but this is a murder enquiry. I already know that Jonathon Black left everything to Helen, and she in turn left everything to Alan Shepherd."

"That's correct." He had become very guarded.

"What I need to know is does anyone else benefit from their deaths?"

"I'll just get the file." I heard the phone being placed upon the desk, the opening and closing of a drawer and the rustling of papers. "There are a few bequests to local organisations. Little amounts, certainly nothing worth killing for."

"So there is nothing out of the ordinary in either will?"

"Nothing."

"What about Alan Shepherd?"

"Alan?"

"Has Alan made a will? Do you know who would benefit if he were to die?"

"You don't think ..." his voice faded to a whisper.

"I'm only pushing theories around, Simon. This bastard is still around and at the moment I have no idea who he is."

"Alan hasn't made a will with me. Though, now that he has inherited a bit of money, it would be a very good idea if he did."

"So, if Alan were to die ..." I stopped. I didn't want to be going here. "If Alan were to die before he made a will, what would happen?"

"I would be a very busy man trying to trace any family of Alan's no matter how distant. Failing that everything would pass to the state."

"So, you can think of no one who would benefit if anything happened to Shepherd?"

"No one. In fact, Jonathon always led me to believe that Alan has no family."

"What about Cat Browning?"

"I'm sorry?" His surprise at my question was evident.

"Do you know of anything that might link her to the Blacks?"

"Nothing at all. Why are you asking?"

"Just curiosity, Simon."

"Remember it killed the cat, Mike." His attempted

joke shocked me into silence and icy fingers ran down my spine. "Mike, are you still there?"

"Sorry, just thinking of something. Look, thanks for your time and your help, Simon. I appreciate it."

"No problems – but – if you have any influence at all over Alan, persuade him to come and see me about a will."

"I will. Good-bye, Simon."

I replaced the phone. So, the motive for the murders wasn't money, the Blacks had not been killed for their estate. Also, Alan wasn't a target because he had inherited, because there was no one who would benefit from his death. Therefore if money wasn't the motive, what was? I had crossed one idea out, now I needed another. I needed some luck.

Grayson informed me that Shepherd had phoned to say that he wouldn't be in, so I spent the rest of the day re-visiting the witnesses to see if they could remember any more details about either the blue van, or the florist's van. The only extra snippet was that the florist's van had been seen driving onto the garage forecourt at about four fifteen. A young man in a leather jacket was also seen in the vicinity at around the same time. The witness hadn't recognised him and the other comment he could make was that he appeared to be clean shaven. The garage had been closed early as Len was taking his wife into Lincoln for a hospital appointment. So either this guy must have local knowledge – even I hadn't known that the garage was closing early – or it was another case of luck being on his side. Whichever way I looked at it, there was no escaping the fact that he was always two steps ahead of me, grinning.

Forty Four

It was a little after six when I arrived at Elderton Manor. The dogs seemed pleased to see me, the sticky slobber all over my hands evidence of their love and affection.

"How are you, lad?"

"OK," he showed me in. He was very quiet and in his eyes I could still see that haunted look. His skin was the colour of chalk.

"Can I do anything? Have you eaten?"

"No and yes," he gave me a thin smile. "Cat cooked me a snack before I drove her to the pub. She's decided to hire me as her personal chauffeur. Not that I mind, I don't like the idea of her walking all the way to The Cat and Fiddle on her own – not at the moment."

"Quite right too. I'd told her to ring me at the station if she needed a lift."

"It was good her being here this afternoon. She helped me sort through some of Aunt Helen's clothes and things. We've got several bags ready to take to the charity shops."

"Good idea."

"I wanted to send the jewellery too, but then I found that I couldn't even bear to look at it. Cat told me to hang onto it – pass it on to my daughter."

"So you should. Your aunt would like to think that you had passed her jewellery on. For the moment, put the boxes in the back of a cupboard somewhere and forget about them until you are ready. Jewellery is a very personal thing – lots of memories attached to it. Just put it away until much, much later."

"OK."

He stood awkwardly in the hall, hands in pockets as he watched his feet kicking at imaginary tufts of carpet.

"Let's make a cup of tea. I'm gasping."

"Er – Sir, can you stay for an hour or so. I came across a large box of papers at the back of the linen cupboard. I need to go through them and you'll know better than me if they are important or not. They look like policies and deeds and stuff."

"Certainly, I've got no other plans. But I thought that you and your aunt went through all the papers when your uncle died."

"We did. We went through it all and made arrangements for everything to be switched into her name. That's why I was surprised to see this box."

"Well, you go and fetch it and I'll bring the tea."

Shepherd's idea of a box and my idea of a box turned out to be very different. The box that I saw when I entered the lounge was not a shoe box, but a large black tin box of the type that I usually associate with bank vaults.

"I thought you said it was a box!" I put the mugs on the coffee table.

"It is."

"No, lad, that's no box, that's a trunk."

As I sat beside him on the floor, he opened it up. As we had expected, at the top there were envelopes full of old insurance polices which had long since expired. It looked as if Helen Black had kept everything not matter how small. There were even receipts for dog food! All of these were put on a pile for burning. However, underneath the first layers of documents we came across little boxes of photographs.

"I don't ever remember seeing these before," Shepherd mused as he examined them.

Spreading them out on the floor in front of us, we gazed at them intently.

"I was never ever shown these. I wonder why? Look!" He picked up one of a smiling group of people. "There's Uncle Jon and Aunt Helen, and these – they're my parents."

I took the photo from him. Helen Black had certainly been a very striking woman in her youth. Looking more closely, I could see that Shepherd had inherited his mother's eyes.

"When was this taken?" I asked.

"Don't know. Is there anything on the back?"

I turned it over – it was blank. Putting it down, my eye was caught by another photograph of the young Helen Black, only this time she was holding a baby. I picked it up.

"Look – here's one of you with your aunt."

Handing it over, I watched as Shepherd examined it. He looked at it closely, then as he turned it over to read the note scribbled on the back, his brow furrowed. He turned it over a second time for an even closer investigation.

"It's not me. The date on the back is three years before I was born."

"Wonder who it is."

"It just says James."

Putting it down with the others we noticed that there were several photos of the same baby with either Helen Black, her husband or the both of them. To all intents and purposes it looked like a set of happy family pictures.

"Any idea who the kid is?"

"None at all." He continued to pour over the photos. "Look at this."

He handed me another photo of Helen, Jon and the baby.

"What about it?"

"That's not Uncle Jon."

Looking more closely I could see that he was right. Except for a slight difference in the shape of the jaw, the two men could have been twins. Both had the same fair hair, and both were of the same build.

"Who is it?"

"No idea."

As Shepherd continued to look over the photos I removed an old biscuit tin from the trunk. Opening it up there were yet more papers to go through. Reaching for the top one I began to read.

"Alan."

Shepherd turned to me with a quizzical look upon his face. I rarely called him Alan.

"You need to see this, lad."

Handing him the document, I watched incomprehension move over his face like a cloud over the sun.

"I had no idea. They never, ever mentioned him."

163

The document was a birth certificate detailing the birth of a child – James Black, son of Jonathon and Helen Black. Shepherd picked up the photos of the baby again.

"This must be him. I wonder what happened."

The next document that I removed from the tin answered his question. It was the child's death certificate. James Black had died at the age of thirteen months. Cause of death was a fractured skull and severe head injuries.

"Oh my God! Poor Aunt Helen."

"Alan!"

I looked at him, holding in my hands several old newspaper clippings, clippings that would turn Shepherd's already fragile world upside down. Silently, I handed them over and let him read them for himself.

"What is this?" He was struggling to make sense of what he was reading. "Uncle arrested for nephew's murder! What is this? I don't understand!"

He threw the clippings down in disgust and held his head in his hands.

"Why did they never tell me any of this? Why keep it a secret? Surely they knew that one day I would find out."

"Maybe it was too painful for them – maybe they didn't want to be reminded of the pain that they had felt. Remember when you came here you were young, and young boys are inquisitive creatures. You would have asked too many questions, not intentionally, but you would have opened up too many wounds. Then, when you were of an age to talk to about such things, maybe they found it too hard to know where to start."

"Uncle Jon had a brother!"

Shepherd was now sitting looking at the photo of the man who was his uncle's brother. He was calmer now.

"What did he do, does it say?"

I took out another pile of clippings and flicked through them.

"According to the reports, Black had been drinking heavily. The baby was crying and he lost his temper. He smashed the child's head against the cot to keep him quiet."

Shepherd was visibly moved and an air of incredulity surrounded us as together, we read through the rest of the clippings.

"How could anyone do that to a baby? To his own nephew?"

I was already reading the next clipping.

"He was found guilty and sentenced to twenty five years."

"So he must be out now."

I flicked over to the next clipping and sighed. "He never came out – look." I handed the clipping over so Shepherd could read for himself the end of the story. A month after he was imprisoned, William Black hanged himself in his cell.

"Sir, did you notice this photo?" Handing the newspaper clipping back to me, he pointed to a figure on the right hand side. It was a photo of William Black's funeral, and standing at the graveside was his heavily pregnant wife, Angela.

"William Black had a child!"

"So," I wasn't sure if this was the right time to ask this question, "this child, wherever it is, will be the new Sir

165

or Lady Black?"

"No – don't you remember what Aunt Helen told you? Uncle Jon's was granted a life peerage for his charity work, it doesn't carry on."

I made some quick calculations. "So this child will be around twenty seven and could even be married with a family."

Shepherd nodded, but I could see that his mind was elsewhere.

"I think we need to track him – or her – down, lad."

His head shot up. "You're not thinking …"

"I'm trying to eliminate all possibilities."

"But that's ridiculous. There's no title to claim. There would be no claim on the estate – he or she would have nothing to gain from murdering Uncle Jon and Aunt Helen."

"Maybe not." I said no more.

As we carried on sorting through the chest, evidence of Helen and Jon's loss came pouring out. Carefully packed to protect them were baby clothes and those precious first curls. Everything was evidence of a life taken too soon and I felt a lump at the back of my throat as memories threatened to resurface. A parent never recovers from the loss of a child.

"Are you OK, Sir?"

"Yes, lad, I'm fine. Look, let me help you clear this lot up and then I'll be off. I'll hang onto these clippings, if that's OK, and see what I can find out."

"You'll be wasting your time, Sir."

"Maybe."

Half an hour later, I sat in my car gazing at the photo that I always kept hidden away in my wallet. The Blacks would have thought that life would never again have any meaning for them. I knew from painful experience that the pain never leaves – it may hide behind corners sometimes, but it remains with you always. No wonder they accepted Shepherd into their home after his parents died; they had all of that bottled up love to share. He had been a very lucky and a much loved boy.

Forty Five

Sleep had been slow to arrive as the feelings awoken
by the discovery of the baby clothes had been
agonisingly painful. Therefore, when the alarm went off
it was very difficult to rouse myself. Not even Ophelia's
morning greetings could lift my mood. As I left the
cottage, she seemed particularly affronted that I had left
my toast and marmalade untouched on the kitchen table.

Grayson was waiting for me when I pulled into the car
park.

"Sorry, Sir, but there has been another sheep attack."

I sighed. Would this never end? "Where?"

"The Dean's farm, bottom of West End."

"What about the patrols?"

"They were driving by regularly on their rounds, but
never saw anything."

"Thanks. If Shepherd comes in, let him know where I
am."

A surprise awaited me at the Dean's small-holding.
Not only had the two sheep been treated gently again,
but there was another clue. For some unknown reason
my guy had collided with a tree in the lane on his way
out. Judging by the damage to the tree, he must have
really battered his van; there was windscreen glass all
around the base of the tree. It was even possible that he
may have been injured – I crossed my fingers and hoped.
However, I knew that it would be useless ringing around
the local hospitals; he was too smart for that.
Nevertheless, a van with no windscreen should be easy

to spot.

By the time I left the Deans, I had yet another set of photos and two more interviews which included the stock phrase, 'we heard and saw nothing'. The only positive thing was that if he was following the same pattern as the previous two murders, he still did not have enough fleeces to fill a crate. Therefore, the next victim was safe – for now.

Back at the station I arranged for all garages and workshops within a twenty mile radius to be contacted about possible damage to a blue van. In the meantime, I retrieved from my wallet, the photos and the newspaper clippings of William Black's pregnant wife. Could this be the clue that I needed? I picked up the phone and dialled.

"Sylvia, it's Mike Malone."

The honey-warm tones of Sylvia Grey, the local registrar, filled my ear.

"Hello, Mike. What can I do for you, unless for the first time ever this is a social call?"

"Sylvia, my love, you know me too well. I'm trying to trace someone and I would very much appreciate your help. Unfortunately it's not someone from this area. I wouldn't ask but it is very important."

"The price will be a drink, Mike."

"If you can do this for me, you can have a meal to go with it."

She laughed, "You're on."

"I'm trying to trace Angela Black, Jonathan Black's sister-in-law."

"Sister-in-law?"

"I was surprised too. It seems that Jonathan Black had a brother, William, who died twenty odd years ago leaving a wife, Angela, who was pregnant at the time of his death."

"Any idea where I might find them?"

"When William died, she was living in Lincoln so it is just possible that she had the baby there."

"So, you want me to search through all the births registered in or around Lincoln at that time?"

"Sorry."

"OK," she laughed again, "I'll see what I can do."

"You are a real angel."

"See you soon, Mike."

"Bye"

The door opened as I put the receiver down and Shepherd entered.

"Morning, lad. Everything OK?"

He sat down. "Fine, I've just dropped Cat off at work." He put a document on the desk in front of me. "I found this after you left."

The document was a will.

"This was written two years before the baby was born."

I read through it quickly. Jonathon had left everything to Helen. However, if she should pre-decease him, or die within three months of him, then everything would pass over to his brother, William – unless of course there were children. "But we know there was a later will. This is worthless."

Looking at Shepherd and at the will in front of me I

remembered Simon's advice.

"Look, lad, I know that this is not actually the right time, but your uncle's solicitor thinks it would be a good idea for you to visit him and make your own will."

"Why?"

"Well, you have inherited a bit of money and you do need to make plans for it in case something …"

"In case I'm next on his list."

"I didn't say that."

"I'll sort something out later. Though who on earth can I leave money to?"

"A good boss!" I winked at him and he laughed.

"Or the cat's home, Sir."

Forty Six

He unloaded the fleeces with some difficulty. The knock on the head was making him feel nauseous and his wrist was extremely painful. He didn't think that it was broken, just badly sprained. Later, he would strap it and take a couple of painkillers, but he needed to sort things out first. Damn! He would now have to find another van – the damage to the blue one was too severe for it to remain inconspicuous.

Locking the barn he got back into the van and with a grimace, he switched on the ignition. A sharp pain shot up his arm and for a moment he thought he was going to vomit. Sitting back, he took several deep breaths and the feeling passed. Slipping the van into gear, he slowly made his way out of the yard.

Two hours later he was lying on his bed waiting for the painkillers to kick in. The van was disposed of, the number plate buried and the tax disc burned. He sucked the blood off his knuckles; the file had slipped several times while he was erasing the serial number from the chassis. What was a drop of spilt blood in return for anonymity?

By four o'clock we had phoned every garage and workshop for miles. No one had a blue van in their workshop. I had expected as much, he would have known that contacting the garages would be top of our 'to do' list. No, he would have disposed of it. In a few days time we would receive a report of an abandoned vehicle, but by then it would be too late.

The phone brought me back to the present.

"Malone."

"Mike, it's Sylvia. Do you have enough money in that wallet of yours to pay for a meal?"

"Of course! What have you found out?"

"Angela Black gave birth to a son, William, in the city hospital. I have her address at the time the birth was registered."

"You are fantastic! I have some contacts in the city, so I'll see if I can pull in a few favours."

She gave me the address. The area was not a very respectable one. Poor woman, she must have been left with nothing. I chatted to Sylvia for a few minutes more, made arrangements to take her to lunch at the end of the week, and then said my good-byes.

The next phone call was to a DI that I had known for nearly ten years. After explaining my reasons for wanting to find Angela Black, he agreed to help. Putting the phone down, I began to feel uneasy. Was this just a wild goose chase? Shepherd certainly thought it was. Should I be spending my time upon more profitable enquiries closer to home? I looked around the office but the shadows were hiding in corners; there was no one to answer me.

Shepherd opened the door and the dogs rushed out to greet me.

"I've brought fish and chips."

"Great! I haven't got around to making anything, still sorting through all of the papers and photos."

I followed him into the kitchen and armed with a bottle

of beer each, we soon polished off the food. I was pleased to see that some of his old spark had returned. He was still not the old Shepherd, but then these things take time and he had had an enormous amount to deal with. Tomorrow, once the funeral was over, he could begin to start looking forward again.

"Have you uncovered anything else of interest?"

"Not really."

I looked over at the photos on the dresser. "You certainly seem to have had an idyllic time growing up here. I've never seen photos brimming with so much joy and happiness."

Shepherd's face clouded over as he followed my gaze and instantly I regretted opening my mouth.

"Who is the other lad – the one with the winning smile?" I pointed to the photo of a very young Shepherd sitting with another boy, both of them showing off their missing front teeth.

The clouds over Shepherd's face thickened. Was I ever going to say anything right?

"That was Jimmy Reed. His dad, Ron, he used to help Uncle Jon. Jimmy and I sort of grew up together. He died of leukaemia when he was eleven. Ron died two years later; he never got over losing Jimmy and he ended up shooting himself. Uncle Jon discovered him and I'll never ever forget the look on his face as he told Aunt Helen and me the news.

"Poor man! What about his wife?"

"She'd walked out when Jimmy was a baby. Jimmy was the glue that held Ron together,"

We fell silent and drank our beers.

"Anyway, Sir, are you going to sit here drinking all night or are you actually going to help me with the rest of these papers?"

The clouds had parted; I followed him into the lounge.

Forty Seven

Cat and I stood as the Vicar entered. Today even the church seemed to be in mourning. The gloom enveloped us and the candles in the dark recesses were just tiny pin-pricks of light. Nowhere was there any comfort or hope.

The Vicar's all too familiar words washed over me as I watched the coffin's slow procession down the nave. Shepherd was the sole mourner and he followed the body of his beloved aunt with his head bowed and his arms held stiffly at his sides. I had offered to walk with him, but he had been determined to do this alone. Watching him take his place in the front pew, alone, I was reminded of another funeral, many years ago, when there had also been a figure sitting alone in the front pew. I felt such sympathy for the lad and for all of his pain, but anger was the over-riding emotion. Anger that I had failed to bring the perpetrator to justice.

The opening notes of 'There's an Old Rugged Cross' immediately brought a lump to my throat. I had known that Shepherd had chosen the hymn as it was one of his aunt's favourites, but I wasn't expecting it to unlock old memories. Once again, I was a nine year old boy hanging onto my father's hand as the words of the hymn came to rest upon my mother's coffin. Cat's hand slipping into mine brought me back to the present and I passed her a tissue which she accepted gratefully.

Half an hour later I was at the graveside supporting Shepherd as he said a final goodbye to the woman who had played such a huge part in his life; Cat had stayed behind with the rest of congregation. As we turned away from the grave, Shepherd took hold of my arm.

"Would you run me home, Sir? I can't face anyone. I just want to be on my own."

"Certainly, I'll just let Cat know where I'm going."

Handing him my car keys, I went off in search of Cat. At first I was unable to spot her and my heart skipped a beat. I was pacing around the churchyard like an anxious parent.

"Mike!"

Turning, I saw her standing underneath one of the horse chestnut trees. With her was the young man who had been with Morris Cutler at Jonathon Black's funeral. I recognised the fedora and the sunglasses. His long black hair was rippling in the breeze. Poser! Struggling to keep the annoyed father expression from my face, I walked over to them.

"Mike," Cat smiled, "this is Christopher Armstrong." He offered me his hand.

"Sprained it playing rugby last weekend," he explained when he saw me taking notice of the heavy strapping on his wrist. I nodded and observed him. Strong jaw line, smartly dressed in a designer suit and ankle length black coat. He certainly liked to draw attention to himself.

"So, how did you know Helen Black?"

"Mike, stop being such a policeman." Cat playfully punched my arm.

"It's OK," Christopher Armstrong turned towards me, smiling at me as if I needed indulging. I was beginning to take a real dislike to this young man. "I work with Jack Cutler. I got to know Jonathon and Helen when I used to come and visit Jack."

I nodded to him and then turned back to Cat.

"I'm taking Alan home, he doesn't feel up to being around people. Do you want a lift to the pub?"

"I'll take you." Armstrong had spoken before Cat had had a chance to open her mouth. She turned to him with a wide smile.

"Thanks, that would be great," she turned to me. "It's OK, Mike, I'll stay here. Give Alan my love."

She resumed her conversation with Armstrong as I walked back to the car. Before my mood had just been sombre, now it was black.

The journey back to Elderton Manor was quiet. Shepherd was too lost in his own grief to notice my mood which pleased me as I didn't want to discuss the subject of the charming Mr Armstrong.

"Do you want me to stay?" I asked as we pulled up.

"Would you be offended if I said no?"

"Of course not, lad. If you need anything, just give me a call. I'll pop in tonight."

"Thanks, Sir. For everything."

Shutting the door he walked across the gravel and unlocked the door. He turned and gave me a pale smile before going into the house, alone. I watched the door close before leaving.

At lunchtime I decided to skip the sandwich and coffee at the station, preferring to make the short drive to The Cat and Fiddle to see Cat. However, as soon as I opened the door I could see that he was still around. Christopher Armstrong. He was seated on a bar stool and was

178

laughing and joking with her. The hat and coat had gone but the sunglasses still remained. Cat noticed me and smiled. Nodding to Mr Armstrong, I placed myself at the opposite end of the bar so that she would have to leave him to talk to me. I felt like a petulant schoolboy, but at that precise moment I didn't care. Looking around, I noticed Bob Archer watching me with a malicious glint of pleasure at my discomfort. For the second time in as many hours, my mood darkened.

"Usual, Mike?"

"Yes please, Cat." I looked across at Armstrong. "You two seem to be getting on very well."

"He's funny. He has so many stories about life in the city."

"When is he leaving?"

"He's not. He's staying with Morris Cutler until after the weekend. He can't play rugby on Sunday because of his wrist and he needs to rest."

"Isn't that nice!" I choked back the sneer so that she wouldn't hear it.

"How's Alan?"

"Not good."

"I'll pop in for five minutes after work. Chris is taking me for a drive this afternoon."

"That's nice. I'm sure that Alan wanted to be alone anyway." The sarcasm escaped into the air before I could stop it and it hung between us. Cat looked at me with hurt in her eyes.

"I'll see you later, Mike." She turned her back and went to rejoin Armstrong, not even giving me the chance to apologize. Damn! I downed my drink in one and headed for the door. Turning to look at her as I left, I caught her eye and mouthed the word 'sorry'. She shrugged her shoulders and looked away. As I slammed the door behind me, I caught sight of Bob Archer laughing.

Back at the station, my pen was making thick, angry marks across my pad; its nib scoring deep gashes into the pure white surface of the paper. Anger was stalking the office waiting for a victim upon which to unleash its power.

"Sir," Grayson poked his head around the door, "there was a call for you from Lincoln while you were out."

"Did you take down the details?"

"No, Sir, I told them to phone again this afternoon."

In the office Anger raised his head and smiled.

"You did what?" I thundered.

"I told them to phone back."

"Have you never heard of initiative?" I was on my feet and leaning ferociously across the desk. "Didn't you even bother to ask them what they wanted?"

"I assumed it was a private matter, Sir." Grayson's face had lost its usual healthy glow.

"Private? Private?" Anger was behind me, cheering me on. "This is a bloody police station, man. We are in the middle of a murder investigation. Didn't it occur to you that they might be phoning with information?"

"Sorry, Sir. I didn't think." Grayson seemed to have shrunk.

Sitting down, I picked up my pen to signal the end of the conversation. Grayson shut the door silently behind

180

him and I heard his footsteps retreating back to the front desk. Anger had already left, his lust fully satisfied. However, my outburst had given me no satisfaction whatsoever.

I was considerably mellower when Grayson put the call from Lincoln through a couple of hours later. Within ten minutes I had an address for Angela Black who was now known as Angela Jackson. She had stayed in Lincoln and was now on her third marriage. Unfortunately the call had given me no information about the child. Putting the phone down I considered my next move. I knew that despite Shepherd's misgivings, I had to go to see her. She might be able to shed light on the murders, give me some details from the past that might be relevant. But one thing I was sure of – I would not involve Shepherd. I would go and see her alone.

Shepherd was in the kitchen when I arrived after work. Although still very pale, he did look a lot better than he had been at the funeral. A stack of sympathy cards, some unopened, were on the table.

"Hope you've got the kettle on."

"I switched it on as soon as I heard your car, Sir."

"Good lad."

I sat down and absentmindedly stroked the dogs who had decided that I needed a bit of attention. "How are you doing?"

"I'll get there. The funeral was a lot harder than Uncle Jon's. I just wanted to get away from everyone. I couldn't stand listening to them all say how sorry they were."

181

"That's only natural."

"Cat popped in to check on me. She had a Christopher Armstrong in tow. Who is he?"

"Apparently a friend of Jack Cutler's from Manchester. He said he got to know your aunt and uncle when he used to visit with Jack."

"Really! Can't say I recall him."

"Are you sure?"

"Not really. The Cutler house was always full of various acquaintances of Jack's. There seemed to be a different crowd every weekend. He might have been one of them. I really don't know."

"Well Cat's certainly fallen for his slick city charms."

"And you haven't?"

"These city types are all the same. Flash cars and fancy clothes. Underneath all of that there is nothing."

"Jealous, Sir?"

"No! I just think he's after a fling with a simple country girl as a change from these sophisticated city girls. When he's had his way with Cat, he'll dump her, head back to the bright lights of the city and she'll end feeling used and abused."

"Cat can take care of herself, Sir."

"Can she? I beg to differ."

"You're sounding like her father. What's next, put her on a curfew?"

I smiled. "Cat's a sweet kid who needs someone to look after her, that's all." Picking up my mug, I drank the tea that Shepherd had placed before me. I decided to change the subject. "I've got an address for William Black's wife, in Lincoln."

182

"Do you really think that this is worth pursuing, Sir?"

"I'm covering all bases, that's all."

"So you will go and see her?"

"I'm going tomorrow."

"I'll stay behind, if that's OK, Sir?"

I breathed a silent sigh of relief. "That's fine. If you feel like popping into the station tomorrow, you could always hold the fort until I get back."

We lapsed into a companionable silence and the only sounds that could be heard were the ticking of the clock and the gentle snores of the two dogs.

"When Cat popped in, she said that she was thinking of moving back to her cottage."

I put my mug down and sighed. "I wish she wouldn't, not until we know who this stalker is. I'd rather that she was here with you."

"I – er – rather think that the reason is Armstrong, Sir. She couldn't really invite him back here, could she?"

"Why not? Oh – I see. Damn! I just don't think it's safe for her yet."

"Cat's a grown woman, Sir."

"She's a vulnerable young woman."

"I'll have a word with her, Sir"

I said nothing; I just picked up my mug and continued to drink. For some reason I felt responsible for Cat Browning. Unknowingly, she had unlocked a door that had been firmly closed for several years and fatherly concern was once more on the prowl.

Forty Eight

By eleven thirty next morning, I was driving down a cul-de-sac on the outskirts of Lincoln. The area had a run-down feel to it; the houses looked tidy, but tired. A young woman was pushing a screaming toddler in a battered pushchair; the child was being totally ignored by its mother who was wearing ear-phones and smoking a cigarette which dripped ash onto the child's hood. All of the cars lining the road were at least ten years old, and many were decorated with varying shades of rust. This was certainly not an affluent area; William Black's widow had evidently fallen upon hard times.

I pulled up as close as I could to number eleven. Double checking that the car was securely locked, I made my way to the front door aware that the curtains of the house next door were parting as the occupant took in my every detail. The garden had more or less been left to its own devices and the small lawn was in serious need of a trim. Even the net curtains hanging at the windows didn't look as if they had been washed for years. The front door of number eleven had been wood-stained in previous years, but that too was showing signs of weathering. I knocked twice.

From behind the door I could hear footsteps approaching, heels echoing on an uncarpeted surface. The door opened.

"Yes?"

"Mrs Jackson?" I offered my warrant card. "Detective Inspector Mike Malone. I was wondering if I could have a word, inside?"

I knew that she must be in her late forties, but she looked at least ten years older. Her face was lined, especially around her lips and her cheeks were hollowed. From the look of her hands, I guessed she was a thirty a day woman at least. Her eyes were a light blue and the deep crow's feet were not, I felt, evidence of a happy disposition.

"What about?" Her hand was still firmly holding the door, the yellow nicotine stains highlighted against the darkness of the wood.

"I'm investigating the murders of Sir Jonathon and Lady Helen Black and I am after some background information."

At the mention of the names a shadow passed fleetingly across her face. The door swung open.

"You'd better come in."

She closed the door behind me and led me into what I supposed was the lounge. Dark red wallpaper covered the walls and a dark brown leather three piece dominated the room. Various photographs in gilt frames were dotted around, but the most striking thing in the room was an ornate bronze clock that stood on the mantelpiece. Even my untrained eye could see that it must have been worth a fortune.

She sat on the edge of the settee and pointed to an armchair. The cushion collapsed underneath me as I sat down; it had obviously seen better days. Picking up a cigarette packet, she removed one, lit it and drew deeply upon it.

"Well, what do you want to know?" Her eyes were cold as she spoke.

"Your late husband, William, was Jonathon Black's younger brother?"

She nodded.

"Was there any ill feeling between them?"

"You must have read the reports, what do you think?" Her laughter was sarcastic.

"After your husband was sentenced, did he try to contact his brother?"

"William told me that he had written to Jon, but he never received a reply. He never did it you know." I tried not to let my shock at her statement show on my face. "The kid fell out of its cot. As Will was asleep, he never noticed, not until it was too late."

I didn't even bother replying. I had read the forensic reports for myself. Her belief in her husband's innocence was laughable.

"I believe that you had a son by William?"

"I gave him away. The Blacks left me with nothing. I couldn't feed myself, let alone a kid. I had him adopted."

This information was unexpected.

"Which authority dealt with the adoption?"

"Lincolnshire."

"Has your son tried to contact you at all?"

"Why all these questions?"

Suddenly it struck me that she had not once asked about either Jonathon Black or his wife. It was as if they were of no concern to her.

"As I said, I just need a little background information – it might help me to solve the murders."

She continued to smoke in silence and I fought the urge to get up and open a window. "He turned up on the

186

door step just after his eighteenth birthday. It was a real shock; he was the image of William."

"What did he want to know?"

"Everything."

"So did you tell him – everything?"

"Of course."

"And how did he take it? How did he react to the fact that his father had been found guilty of murdering a baby, and he had committed suicide in jail?" I didn't feel inclined to be nice.

"OK."

I doubted that very much. If it had been me, I would have been appalled, devastated and angry.

"Can you tell me where to find him?"

"No."

"Is that no you can't or no you won't?"

For the first time since my arrival I could see some sign of emotion. There was a flicker pain in her face.

"He never came back. Said he would be back the next day, but never came. That was eight years ago. Ashamed of his own flesh and blood, I expect. Can't say I blame him."

"What is his name, presumably it isn't Black?"

"William Browning."

My pen froze in mid air and I shivered. I didn't like coincidences.

"So Browning is the name of the family that adopted him?" I was struggling to keep the anxiety from my voice, but she was too disinterested to notice my fight to remain calm.

"Apparently."

"Do they live here in Lincoln too?"

"They did then."

"What did your son look like?"

"William, I suppose, with longer blond hair."

"You don't happen to know his shoe size, do you?"

She raised her head and looked at me as if she was really seeing me for the first time. Suddenly, I realised that I could think of no more questions. This shell of a woman had no part in this horror in which I was immersed. It was her son that I needed to speak to. Could there be a connection between him and the murders? And Cat? Was he also connected to her?

I stood and returned my pad to my jacket pocket.

"Well, thank you very much for your time. You've been a great help."

Angela Black/Jackson shrugged her shoulders and rose to show me out. As she shut the door behind me, I wondered again at her total lack of interest in the deaths of her former brother-in-law and his wife.

Forty Nine

It was two fifteen when I walked into the station. I nodded to the constable at the front desk and made straight for my office. Sitting down I called the switchboard and asked them to get the number of Lincolnshire Social Services. By the time a further ten minutes had elapsed, I had passed on all the relevant information to them. All I could do now was sit and wait for them to locate the details of the family that had adopted William Black.

"Sir?"

A young constable entered the office hesitantly.

"What is it, lad?"

"Message from Alan Shepherd, Sir. There has been a fleecing at Harold Chambers' farm. He has taken the team and they are there now. He asked me to tell you that he would give you a full report when he returned."

"OK, thank you."

He left and I let out the breath that I had been holding. He already had four fleeces. How many had he taken this time? There had been eight in the previous two crates. I prayed that he had not yet reached his magic number. I needed more time!

Forty minutes later Shepherd bounded into the office, looking a lot brighter than I had seen him for some time.

"This is good, Sir."

"Sit down, lad."

"Well, the good news is that the sheep, Florrie, is unharmed. The even better news is that he never finished the job."

I stared at him, confusion circling my head like a squadron of tiny paper aeroplanes.

"Say again."

"Harold disturbed him. He had heard a vehicle in the lane so he went out to investigate. His dog ran ahead of him into the field and disturbed him. Florrie has a very lop-sided look to her now – definitely not the height of sheep couture."

He grinned, evidently pleased with himself. Sensing that there was even more to come, I settled back and made myself comfortable.

"As soon as the dog ran into the field, our chap rushed out. Harold didn't get a good look at him, but he did see long, blond hair. And, he also saw him drive away – in a white van whose registration ends in forty five."

"Excellent news. He didn't get his fleece, the description of the long hair matches other descriptions, and, we now have something for the lads to look out for – a white van and a partial registration. Hopefully, he will assume that Harold was too far away to get a good look and he will not decide to dump it."

Shepherd sighed contentedly, pleased with his day's work. The spark had come back into his eyes, and the thirst for the job was returning. Looking closely at me, he suddenly straightened up and the smile left his face as he asked his question.

"Did you see her?"

I nodded. "Life has certainly not been good to her. Anyway the journey has given me a serious headache."

"Travelling can do that."

"That's not what I meant. She had the kid, William,

adopted – didn't keep it. He tracked her down when he reached eighteen but she has seen nothing of him since."

"Do you believe her?"

"Yes."

"And?"

I took a deep breath. "Firstly when she last saw him eight years ago, he had longish blond hair. Secondly, his name was changed when he was adopted. He is not William Black, he is William Browning."

Shepherd was speechless. As he stared at me, I could see millions of thoughts rushing around in his brain, all of them clamouring to be heard. When he finally did speak, it was in no more than a whisper.

"Is there a connection?"

"I don't know. I've contacted the adoption agency in Lincoln and they are pulling up the file for me."

We both gazed at out fingers, not daring to read in each other's faces the thoughts that were wanting to emerge from the darkness.

"Cat has never spoken to me of a brother," Shepherd finally said.

"Nor to me. When she told me her life story, it was only peopled with deserting father figures."

"Same here. It has got to be a coincidence – hasn't it?"

"I hope so, lad. I hope so."

I picked up my pen and doodled on my pad, hoping that the little pencil animals would bring me some comfort.

"Did Armstrong stay the night with her?"

"Sir, that is none of our business."

"Did he?" I was fiercer than I intended and the shock

registered on Shepherd's face.

"I think so."

I was fighting to contain my anger, "She needs to be either staying with you or with me – not offering her bed to any good-looking stranger who happens to be passing."

"Sir, she's twenty two."

"We don't know what William Browning is after. She could be in danger."

"And we don't know if it is William Browning."

"My fingers itch."

"To hit her? I've read Romeo and Juliet too, Sir."

I looked at him, feeling my anger abate.

"No, my instincts are telling me that he is connected to everything. There are too many coincidences flying around for him not to be."

"OK then, level with Cat and let her make up her own mind. She isn't a fourteen year old Shakespearean heroine that you can order around."

I nodded and Shepherd left me. Looking down at my pad, I saw smiling, leering faces everywhere, and in the centre of them a tiny, crouching figure; the figure of a very frightened girl, a girl all alone and defenceless.

Ophelia and I were sitting together in the warm firelight; the scent of roasted garlic still hung in the air. We were in the streets of Verona, witnesses to a street fight, and as Mercutio lay dying, the phone rang.

"Malone."

"Sir, it's Shepherd."

"Hello, lad. Is everything aright?"

"Fine. I've been down to the pub to see Cat. After a long chat, she's moving back in with me tonight."

"That's good. How much did you tell her?"

"I just said that we were concerned for her safety and I would explain everything tonight."

"And Armstrong?"

"He's back in Manchester. Though he is coming down again at the weekend. Am I to tell her everything, Sir?"

"Yes. Also, try and find out as much as you can about her family – we need to see if there is a link."

"Will do. I'll see you in the morning, Sir."

"Have a good night, and thank you."

"Night, Sir."

I put the phone down, pleased that Cat would not be in her cottage, alone. The fear that she was the next victim would not leave me. There was no logic to my fear, just a gnawing in my stomach that would not cease.

A chirp from the sofa reminded me that Ophelia and I still had a story to finish. As I turned towards her, she gazed at me with her liquid green eyes, waiting for me settle back onto the sofa so that she could climb onto my knee.

"Come on, Princess, let's see what Romeo does next."

Fifty

My doodles of the frightened girl were waiting for me when I arrived in my office the next morning. In the cold light of day, they seemed even more appalling; the vulnerability of the victim as the killers were closing in was too much to witness. I ripped it off my pad and crushed it in my hands, I couldn't stand to look at it a moment longer. Abandoned, it lay at the bottom of the waste paper bin.

Shepherd was not going to be in till later as he had an appointment with Simon about the Black's affairs, so I took a deep breath and turned to another pile of brown envelopes that were waiting for my attention. Opening the post, I found the usual demands for statistics and reports; there was nothing to help me with my quest to apprehend William Browning. I turned my attention to the overflowing crime-board. Was William Browning really the person behind all of this death and suffering, or was I condemning him without trial and jury?

The phone rang. By the time I had replaced the receiver, there was a smile on my face; I had an address for the parents William Browning.

"Grayson!"

The familiar face peeped around the door.

"I'm off to Lincoln. Tell Shepherd when he comes in that I'm going to see the parents."

"Yes, Sir."

As I made my way down this cul-de-sac, I couldn't help but notice the differences between these houses and those in the street where Angela Jackson lived. The wealth of these residents was evident; the front gardens to the properties were all beautifully landscaped, and everywhere there were double garages. I found the house and pulled up. Immediately the curtains of the house opposite twitched and as I turned around I caught a glimpse of grey hair. I smiled to myself; the houses may look different, but people never change. As I walked towards the house, I found that although superficially it was like its neighbours, upon closer examination it needed a little care and attention. Stray blades of grass were beginning to poke their noses out between the cracks in the paving slabs and the paintwork on the front door was showing the first signs of age. The vase adorning the front window had once been full of vibrant flowers, now they looked brown and decaying. I knocked.

From inside, I heard a dog barking and the sound of an interior door closing muffled the sound. As the front door opened, I found myself looking into the face of a not unattractive woman, possibly in her late forties. Her brown hair was beginning to grey and her face was brought to life with laughter lines and a pair of sparkling eyes.

"Mrs Browning?"

"I used to be, I'm Mrs Summers now."

I produced my warrant card, which she took and studied carefully.

"Doesn't do you justice, Mr Malone." She laughed as she handed it back to me. "What appears to be the problem?"

"I was wondering whether I could talk to you about your – er – ex-husband and your son, William."

The sparkling lights vanished from her eyes as she opened to door to allow me in. Closing the door she led me into the lounge which was curiously bare of family photos. I had expected to see holiday snaps and wedding photos, the mementoes of family life. I could hear barking from behind a closed door as the dog sensed a stranger in his house.

"Rosie – shh! Please sit down."

I settled myself into a beige armchair and allowed the plump cushion to soothe a back stiff from driving. I watched her as she settled herself opposite me, sitting nervously at the edge of the chair.

"You said that you wanted to know about David and William. Why?"

The unhappiness on her face took me by surprise; for some reason I had been expecting happy families.

"I believe that you adopted William as a baby. Is that correct?"

She nodded. "Do you know anything of his birth parents?"

"Nothing. I know that William was trying to trace them, but it all came to nothing."

"Did he tell you that?"

She looked up, questioningly. "He said that he couldn't find them."

I sighed. Yet again I was going to be the bad guy as I exposed another liar.

"I'm sorry, but I have information that he made contact with his birth mother."

"So he lied to me." The look on her face was not one of hurt, but of resignation. "Why doesn't that surprise me?"

"William's parents are – were William and Angela Black. William Black was jailed for murdering his nephew and he committed suicide in prison shortly before William was born."

Shock and disbelief covered her face like a mask.

"That's dreadful."

"His mother gave him up for adoption as soon as he was born."

I watched her as she settled back into the chair, her eyes misting over with the memories that I knew she would now share with me.

"He was a lovely baby, so gentle and loving. Blonde curls and a winning smile. He was a normal little boy and we were a really happy family."

"You said were."

"Everything changed when my husband, David, walked out. William was five. He changed overnight from a sunny, lively little boy to a withdrawn and sullen stranger. But worst of all, he became cruel. He took great pleasure in inflicting pain on others – I suppose psychologists would say that it was his way of easing his own."

"In what way was he cruel?"

"The school bully – tormenting those weaker than himself. We moved him from three different primary schools and he was expelled from secondary school at fourteen."

"What was his relationship with you like after your

husband left?"

"He blamed me. He made my life a misery; rude, abusive, sadistic. I know that sounds strong, but he used to enjoy seeing me cry. I know it sounds awful, but part of me was really glad when he packed his bags and left."

"When was that?"

"Soon after he turned eighteen."

"That would be around the time that he contacted his birth mother."

"Around the time when he told me that he couldn't find her," she smiled wryly.

"What happened to your husband?"

"He set up home with his secretary after she got pregnant. He jumped at the chance of having his own kid, as unhappily I was unable to oblige him in that area. He married her as soon as the divorce came through but I heard that he walked out on her too."

My palms were beginning to sweat. "Do you know whether the child was a boy or a girl?"

"A girl."

Another coincidence? Cat's father had walked out on her. David Browning had walked out on his second wife and daughter. Was it possible that this was Cat's father?

"Don't suppose you know their names?"

"The secretary was called Sheila, the little girl was Catherine."

My heart was pounding so loudly that I was sure that she could hear it.

"What was William's reaction to the news that his father had a daughter?"

198

"He hated her, and Sheila. We didn't come across them very often, but when he did he would scream and shout at them. It would really upset me."

"Have you seen him recently?"

"He still remembers birthdays and Christmas and I even get a visit. He brings a present and a few choice insults, stays maybe an hour and then he leaves again."

"Where is he now? Do you know?"

"No – he won't let me have his phone number. I don't even know if he has a job."

"Do you happen to have a recent photo?"

She stared directly at me, challenging me.

"Why exactly are you here, Inspector?."

I swallowed. "William Black's brother, Jonathon, whose baby William's father killed, has been murdered. In fact both Jonathon and his wife have been murdered."

"And you think William has something to do with the murders?" She was horrified.

"I don't know. I am trying to eliminate all possibilities. Do you happen to have a recent photograph?"

She got up, went to a drawer and pulled out a silver frame.

"This was taken eighteen months ago. My sister was here when he turned up for his biannual visit. She insisted that a photo be taken to celebrate the occasion of my birthday."

Slowly, I turned my gaze upon the photo for my first glimpse of William Browning. I was expecting to see the devil incarnate; what I saw a smiling young man. Blonde hair curled over his collar, but with piercing blue eyes that were as cold as steel. His smile might have seemed warm and charming, but it certainly didn't extend to his eyes. "Can I hang onto this?"

"I'd rather you didn't."

"Look, I'll get a copy made and I'll send the original straight back. Is that OK?"

She was silently studying her nails,

"Is that a promise?" she said quietly.

"Of course, you have my word." I reached over and patted her hand.

"Even after everything, I do still love him you know. Even after all of the cruelty, I do still love him."

I nodded.

"Inspector – do you think he is involved?"

"I don't know."

She nodded sadly. "They always blame the parents, don't they? If it is him, everyone will blame me, won't they?"

I patted her hand. Not wanting to lie to her, I chose to say nothing.

The drive back gave me plenty of time for contemplation. Was William Browning really the murderer? The eyes in the photo made me think that he was – they were totally devoid of emotion. I sighed and at that moment heard a cacophony of horns. My momentary lack of concentration had almost resulted in a collision – I had sailed through a red light. I put my hand up to acknowledge my error and found myself looking into the face of Dan Marshall. He wound his window down and grinned.

"D.I. Malone! You really must be more careful, you know. You're setting a bad example to other road users."

"Afternoon, Dan. Sorry about that – a lot on my mind."

"Take care, mate."

He pulled away leaving me sitting, rather obviously, in the middle of the road feeling rather stupid, Without wasting anymore time, I put the car back into gear and headed for the station.

Shepherd was at the front desk when I arrived, busy taking details from an elderly lady who had lost her cat. He looked up as I walked through and gave me a thumbs up. Evidently he had found something out. So had I!

Shepherd came into the office half an hour later, carrying two mugs of tea.

"Old ladies and cats! What would we do without them?"

He put the mugs down and pulled up a seat before taking out his notebook.

"I spoke to Cat. Her mum, Sheila, still lives in Lincoln. She hasn't seen her dad, David, since he left them."

I folded my hands around my mug.

"I saw the woman who adopted William. Her husband, David, married his secretary, Sheila. He later left Sheila and their daughter Catherine."

Shepherd's face was a mixture of shock and surprise. "So Cat's real dad adopted William?"

"It certainly seems that way. Apparently he hated Sheila and her. His mum told me how he would scream and hurl abuse whenever he saw them. She also said that as soon as David left, he turned into a sadistic monster of a child."

Taking the photo that she had given me from my jacket, I handed it over to Shepherd.

"He looks so like Uncle Jon, except for the eyes," he mused. He raised his head and looked at me. "This means that Cat is probably next on his list, doesn't it?"

"It certainly looks that way. This all seems to be about revenge. Revenge on your uncle and aunt because he believed that they are … were responsible not only for his father's death but also for his mother rejecting him by giving him away. Revenge on Cat because she is the reason that the father that he adored left."

"What do we do?"

"Tell her, we have to."

"She needs protecting."

"Definitely. She needs to be at Elderton with you. Damn Armstrong! The last thing she needs at the moment is a relationship to make things difficult."

Shepherd sighed. "Elderton is a big house. I suppose I can grit my teeth and allow her to 'entertain" him there if she wishes to. I might not like the guy, but at least there will be two of us in the house to protect her."

"I will arrange for one of the lads to trail her as well. That way she can be watched when she goes to and from work, and she can even be watched while she is there."

"Well, Sir, I don't think there will any shortage of volunteers to sit in a pub all night."

Shepherd grinned and I, too, had no choice but to share the joke. However the smiles soon died on our faces as the reality of the danger that Cat was in swam back to the surface of our thoughts.

"I'll go back and catch her before she leaves for the

pub." Shepherd stood and headed for the office door. "He won't get near her if I have anything to do with it, Sir."

"We'll catch him, lad. We now know who we are looking for – it's just a matter of time."

As Shepherd's footsteps echoed across the station, I photocopied the photograph of William Browning and placed it in the centre of the crime-board. Standing back I looked at it and a shiver ran down my spine. Even in black and white his blue eyes seemed to have a disturbing quality to them; cruel, cold. Where was he?

The Cat and The Fiddle was relatively quiet when I arrived at seven thirty. At home I had found it difficult to settle; nothing was holding my attention – all thoughts kept drifting towards Cat and my fears for her safety. She was talking to Jim Wallace, but the light had gone from her face. She looked paler and her smile was not as bright.

"Evening, Jim. Cat." I sat myself on the stool beside Jim. "Can I get you another, Jim?"

"I'll have another half, thanks."

"A half for Jim, Cat, and a whisky for me."

Her smile was forced; she pulled Jim's pint and placed it on the bar in front of us, together with my whisky. I handed her the money.

"How are you, Cat?"

She leaned over the bar so that she could not be overheard. "What Alan said, is he really after me?"

I took hold of her hand.

"We don't know, love, but we are not going to take

203

any chances. We're not going to let him get within ten feet of you. Alan and I will look after you and," I nodded in the direction of Constable Flowers who was drinking his pint in the corner, "we'll have someone watching over you all the time."

"I'm scared."

"We'll look after you, honest."

The tapping of an empty beer glass at the other end of the bar interrupted our conversation. Cat tried to smile at me, and then left to serve her customer. Picking up my glass, I went over to join Flowers.

Fifty One

He smiled as he put the phone down. A weekend at Elderton Manor. He couldn't have planned it more perfectly himself.

The news came in at eight thirty the next morning. I had barely been in the station for half an hour and had been feeling positive as William – if it was him – had not yet added to his stock of fleeces. However, Grayson's report set all of my internal alarms ringing.

The Spicer's had been targeted again but this time it was worse. Their remaining two sheep had been fleeced and killed.

Getting into my car I guessed that he now had six fleeces; another attack would bring him up to his magic number and then he would start looking for Cat. As I started the engine, I saw Shepherd walking across the yard. I wound down my window.

"Jump in, lad. The Spicer's farm has been hit again. Two more sheep – both dead"

I could see by his face that he was also calculating how many fleeces William Browning now had in his collection. He got in beside me and neither of us spoke a word.

The Spicers were once again sitting in their kitchen but this time despair was scratched onto their faces.

"I'm really sorry, Sam" I said as I shook his hand. "Can you tell me anything all?"

He shook his head and the only sounds I heard were the ticking of the clock and Judy Spicer's gentle sobs.

"Tyre tracks across the field – nothing else."

Nodding to Shepherd, I sat down opposite Samuel Spicer. Shepherd left to go to examine the field.

"Any ideas when it happened, Sam?"

"I'd checked the gate about eleven thirty, just before I went to bed. Found them at six thirty. Bastard!" He spat the word out; his hatred for the person who could commit such atrocities upon gentle dumb animals was plain to see.

"Mrs Spicer, did you hear anything?"

Judy Spicer shook her head, she was unable to speak.

Patting her hand and nodding to Sam, I left them to their grief and went to find Shepherd.

I was totally unprepared for the horror that awaited me in the field. Blood seemed to be bubbling up from the earth itself, to be emerging as tiny red droplets and expanding outwards. In the midst of this turbulent sea, the pale bodies of two sheep were floating, bobbing along and seeking a safe haven that would never be theirs. Each one had had her throat slit. Dan Marshall pulled himself wearily to feet when he saw me approaching.

"Nasty business, Mike."

"What have you got to tell me?"

"Both killed after fleecing – had to be otherwise the fleeces would have been ruined."

"Why?" I was incredulous. "What possible reason could he have had to slaughter them?"

"Sadistic pleasure – I can think of no other reason. He certainly seems to have lost it this time. He didn't just slit their throats, he almost took their heads off. From what I can see, the fleeces were taken off very carefully. That should have been it. He should have packed them away and left, but he didn't. For a reason that we may never get to understand, he decided to savagely murder them. Something must really have pissed him off." Dan was visibly upset and angered by the carnage at his feet.

I shook my head in disbelief, but inside my heart was pounding. The last thing I needed was for him to suddenly to develop a violent streak – not when Cat's life was at stake. Shepherd joined us.

"A long black hair, Sir. It was stuck to one of the bodies."

"How long?"

He held it up and stretched it between his gloved fingers.

"Shoulder length, I should guess."

"Bag it."

I turned away, unable to look upon the slaughter of the innocents any longer. Back in the car, I rested my head upon the steering wheel. Cat's life was in danger; after all, he had nearly completed his collection of eight fleeces. He had the upper hand and I was powerless to stop him. The door opened and Shepherd got in beside me.

"We won't let him get her, Sir."

Raising my head, I turned on him.

"And how are we going to stop him? Pray tell me! What are we going to do? Lock her in the cells until such a time as we manage to catch him. And, how are we going to catch him? We have nothing to go on. We have witnesses who say he is blond but we now have a black hair. So who are we looking for? And, where do we look? Is he William Browning or have I got that wrong as well? Tell me! What are we going to do?" My voice was a lot louder and a lot harsher than I had intended, and I instantly regretted my outburst. "Sorry, lad. It's not your fault, it's just that I feel so damned useless."

"We can't let him win, Sir."

"We won't. We won't."

Switching the engine on, I turned the car and we headed away from the bloodshed and made our way back to the station.

Fifty Two

As he stacked the fresh fleeces into the crate, he smiled. He would soon have achieved his goal – all three of them would have been dealt with. It couldn't come soon enough. Six fleeces would be enough this time – that would catch that stupid copper out. He thought back over his evening's work, and the killing of the sheep. He hadn't set out to kill the sheep. However, his blood lust had suddenly returned as he had been snipping at the wool. He had suddenly wanted to breathe in the metallic scent of warm blood again. He had wanted to watch as the brilliant red liquid glittered in the moonlight. And after all, they were just sheep – dumb, stupid animals. They didn't even try and put up a fight, for God's sake.

I had just made myself a cup of coffee and was preparing to sit down with Ophelia and the week's papers so that I could catch up on all the news that I had missed, when the doorbell rang. I swore under my breath; Saturday mornings were my time to relax. Grumbling, I put the mug down and made for the door, ready to send away either salesman or Girl Guide with a flea in their ear.

"Morning, Sir."

The sight of Shepherd at the door took me by complete surprise. His jacket collar was turned up and his hands were burying themselves into his pockets in an attempt to keep the cold wind out. He had the air of someone who had lost a fiver and found a farthing.

"What can I do for you, lad? No trouble is there?"

"I was just passing and I …."

"Come on in, lad." I stood back to let him pass. "Fancy a coffee?"

His manner brightened as soon as his foot hit my doormat. It was as if a weight had suddenly been lifted off his shoulders.

"It's good of you, Sir. I just didn't know where to go."

I followed him into the kitchen and watched him as he unbuttoned his jacket and sat down. He relaxed into my kitchen and Ophelia immediately jumped onto his knee, sensing that this was someone who needed a lot of fuss. Placing his coffee in front of him, I sat down and waited.

"I just had to get out, Sir. I know I said that Armstrong could stay – but – I feel like a gooseberry in my own home. I just don't like him, he's not right for her."

"When does he go back?"

"He's here until Sunday night. Oh, God!"

"Well, I'm sure he'll take care of Cat."

"Oh, he's certainly taking care of her." His face twisted with a bitterness that I had never seen before.

"Jealous, lad?"

"No! He's just not her type. You were right. What does a city type like him see in Cat anyway? She can't be in the same league as his usual conquests."

"You're being a bit harsh on Cat."

"I don't … you know what I mean. Cat isn't sophisticated like these city girls in their designer labels and their Jimmy Choo shoes. Cat's a sweet, country girl. There is nothing false about her, she's as natural as the air I breathe."

I smiled knowingly. No he wasn't jealous – of course

not! Not at all. "Unfortunately for Cat, my hunch is that it will not last long. He's after a change of scene, a quick fling and then he will return to his stable of thoroughbreds."

"Good!"

We drank our coffee in a companionable silence watching as Ophelia gracefully rolled onto her back to encourage Shepherd to rub her tummy. She was one contented cat.

"Is that all that's bothering you, lad?"

Shepherd put his mug down.

"Yes – no. Well, I spent last night reading Aunt Helen's diaries and I wish that I hadn't."

I drank my coffee and waited for him to continue.

"The dairies date back to the time of the trial. Reading about her pain was dreadful. Anyway, it appears that Black's widow contacted her after Black's suicide and told her that as far as she was concerned they had killed William. She wanted nothing to do with them ever again and she promised that they would never see their nephew. Poor Aunt Helen. It would have been a real slap in the face for her, because you know as well as I do that she was the sort of person who would have moved heaven and earth to help this woman and her child."

"So, I don't expect Angela Black had anything nice to say about either of them when Browning went to see her."

"Exactly – you can see why he is so determined to take revenge on everyone that he feels contributed to his misfortune. He's killed Uncle Jon and Aunt Helen to avenge his father. Now he's after Cat because the man who adopted him, who he loved as a father, preferred her to him."

"And that is why you are putting up with Armstrong – so you can keep an eye on her."

"I know." He shuffled in his chair and Ophelia glared at him, telling him to sit still because she was very comfortable, thank you very much.

"Have you made a decision about the house yet?" I decided that it was time to change the subject.

"I'm going to keep it. It'll mean a squeeze in the old finances, but I can't sell it. I'm going over to the cottage later to start sorting things out – what to keep and what to sell. Then I'll give notice to my landlord."

"Good lad, it's the right decision."

He scowled at me. "It's all right for you, Sir. You won't be the one living on bread and water for the next twenty years."

"Neither will you, lad. I'll treat you to a tin of beans occasionally."

It was good to see him laugh.

On Sunday, I woke up and decided to pop into the station. I had had a bad night's sleep; something was once again lurking at the back of mind, hiding in corners, determined not to be caught. Something important. Sitting at my desk, I once again went through all of my notes, all of my reports, everything. The face of William Browning was taunting me from the crime-board, his piercing eyes following my every move, mocking me. Blonde hair, tall, scruffy – the description of the man in the pub and Cat's stalker. Long blonde hair, could it have come from an expensive wig worn when he killed Helen Black. It had not been a synthetic fibre. Now we had a long black hair. That was the anomaly. That was the piece of evidence that was making me uneasy. It didn't fit in with everything else. Added to that was the savage slaughter of the Spicer's sheep. He'd never shown such naked sadism before – why now?

I was scared. For the first time in my life I was scared of failing, scared that a beautiful young woman would die a brutal death because of my inadequacy.

I needed air and decided to walk to The Cat and Fiddle for lunch to check that Cat was safe. The morning mist was still sticking stubbornly to the rooftops, and there was a bitter chill in the air. Hopefully, Bob Archer would have his log fire blazing away. I opened the door and the smell of wood smoke invaded my nostrils. Wonderful.

Cat was clearing glasses and Shepherd was sitting in the corner with a plate of sausage and mash. I nodded to him and went over to Cat.

"Hello, Mike."

"Where's the boyfriend?"

"He's gone to see the Cutlers. He's picking me up when I finish and we're going for a drive to find a nice, quiet little tea shop."

"Good for you."

She put a half of bitter down in front of me.

"You did want your usual, didn't you?"

"Of course, now what do I owe you?"

I took my beer and went to join Shepherd.

"I thought you were on a diet of bread and water?"

He laughed. "That starts tomorrow. I'm having my last taste of real food before the penny-pinching starts."

"Everything OK at the house?"

"I'll be glad when he's gone. There is definitely something about him that irritates me. It's his expression, I'm sure he's laughing at me."

"Has he ditched the sunglasses yet?"

"Yes and no, he says he has to wear them when his contact lenses irritate, but I just think he's a poser"

"As I said, lad, city types are all false and puffed up."

"If I buy you another half, Sir, do you fancy joining me for a spot of packing this afternoon?"

"Make it a pint and you're on."

By six o'clock I was exhausted. Between us, Shepherd and I had cleared two rooms and his shed. After two trips to Elderton Manor we decided to call it a day and supper was pie and chips at The Cat and Fiddle. Armstrong was sitting at the bar talking to Cat.

"They just don't look like a couple, do they, lad?"

"I know what you mean. It's like hanging the Mona Lisa in a betting shop. They just don't belong together."

"What time is he leaving?"

"Not until the morning! A change of plan – he's staying another night and leaving first thing."
Shepherd's eyes were flashing with what looked like real hatred. Something that I had never seen before. "And I expect he'll be back next weekend."

"You really don't like him, do you?"

"For someone who came to both funerals because he had supposedly got to know Uncle Jon and Aunt Helen well when he used to stay in the village, he certainly goes out of his way to poke fun at their memory. Little comments to Cat about the furniture, about the decoration, about the house when he thinks that I'm not listening. He came as a voyeur – nothing else."

I didn't interrupt him, I gave him the opportunity to release his pent up frustrations.

Back at the cottage later, I thought about what Shepherd had said. If Armstrong had been close to the Blacks, he would certainly have treated their home, and Shepherd, with a little more respect. I decided to go to see the Cutlers in the morning.

Fifty Three

Raising himself up on his elbow, he watched her as she slept. She could have been a Russian icon with her red hair surrounding her pale face like a halo. He traced the outline of her lips with the tip of his finger and she stirred slightly. Sighing, he carefully opened the drawer of the bedside cabinet and removed the syringe.

"Such a pity, Miss Browning. I could have fallen for you."

Gently brushing her hair to one side, he stabbed the needle into her neck. She started, opened her eyes and immediately fell back onto the pillow once again – her breathing slower and deeper than before.

"Perfect," he whispered, and bending over her, he kissed her lips. "Goodnight, sweet angel."

It was ten o'clock and I was not in a good mood. Sitting at my desk surrounded by pointless memos asking for breakdowns of spending and overtime, I cursed the way that my job was being strangled by endless paperwork. Filling in returns was not what I came into the force for, it was to catch criminals. I should be putting murderers behind bars, not stuffing reports into envelopes. Angrily, I pushed them to one side.

"Grayson!"

He put his head around the door.

"Sir?"

"Did Shepherd say what time he'd be in?"

"Not exactly, Sir. He said he had a meeting at the

solicitors, and then he was going to see his landlord about his cottage. He thought he would be in by mid-day."

"I'm going out. If he returns, tell him to wait, I won't be long."

"Sir."

Grabbing my jacket, I left the station and made for the High Street. The sky was white, not a patch of blue to be seen. I pulled my jacket closer to me as the cold air nipped my fingers. As I walked, I watched those around me; mothers pushing toddlers, elderly gentlemen leaning on their walking sticks to chat upon street corners. All were safe in their own little worlds and not one of them had the problems that were on my shoulders. Didn't any of them care that a brutal murderer was on the loose and ready to strike again?

Reaching the butchers, I opened the door, listening to the metallic clicking of the bell. Morris Cutler had his back to the door and was slicing steaks from a bloody carcass on the cutting board; he turned at the sound of the bell.

"D.I. Malone. What can I get you?"

"I'm just here for a chat, Morris."

He put down his cleaver and wiped his hands on his apron, leaving bloody streaks upon the white cloth. It always amused me to observe that his face was constantly the colour of the steaks that ornamented his front window.

"It's about Christopher Armstrong, Morris."

"Who?"

"Jack's friend from Manchester. He came to the

funerals of Jonathon and Helen Black." I nervously ran my finger around my collar.

"Oh, him. Don't know a lot about him. Jack phoned us and asked if we could put him up when he came to the funerals."

"So, you'd never met him until the day of Jonathon Black's funeral?"

"No. He arrived the night before and came along with us."

"So he'd never visited before?"

"Never."

"So how did he know the Blacks?"

"Said he was a friend of the family from years back. I say, D.I.Malone, are you OK?"

I had felt the colour draining from my face and my heart rate increasing as Morris had been speaking. Armstrong had never known the Blacks. That was why Shepherd hadn't remembered him. It wasn't because Jack Cutler had a wide circle of friends, it was because he had never ever set foot in the place – until now. My mouth went dry as the truth slowly dawned on me. Christopher Armstrong and William Browning were the same person. The long black hair found at the Spicer's – it was Armstrong's. And he was with Cat. I had given her to him, gift-wrapped. God, what a fool I was. Mumbling my thanks to Morris I ran back to the station.

"Sir?"

Grayson was looking at me with concern as I pushed the door open, gasping for breath with my heart threatening to burst through my ribcage.

"It's Armstrong." I gasped.

218

"Sir, sit down. Let me get you a drink."

"No time. We need to find Cat Browning."

Turning, I stumbled back out of the door with Grayson following on my heels. The car engine was started and I was leaving the yard before Grayson had had chance to close the door.

"Armstrong is William Browning. He is with Cat."

The blaring of a horn as I drove straight through a red light, made me catch my breath. I swung the car around the corners until I came to Elderton Manor. Switching off the engine, I motioned to Grayson that he should follow. Keeping close to the hedges we made our way up the drive.

Shepherd's car was in the drive, and the house looked silent. I ran across the gravel, and with sweating palms I hammered on the door.

"Cat! Cat!"

Only the barking of the dogs could be heard.

"Round the back."

Together, Grayson and I ran around to the back of the house. Everything was just as Shepherd and I had left it last night. Nothing had been disturbed. I put my hands on the wall and hung my head. Grayson's hand touched my arm.

"It's nearly eleven, sir. She'll be at the pub."

"Of course, you're right."

In silence we walked back to the car and in a calmer frame of mind I drove us to The Cat and Fiddle. It was still not quite opening time, so we made our way to the back. Grayson knocked while I hung back. The door swung open ferociously.

"And what time do you call this?"

Bob Archer stopped as soon as he saw us.

"Oh, it's you! I thought you were Cat – she's late."

My heart missed a couple of beats.

"She's not here?"

"That's what I just said. She's late."

"Hasn't she phoned you?" I was desperate for some news, any news.

"No. Now if there's nothing else, I've got work to do as I am now single-handed."

As he shut the door in our faces, Grayson turned to me.

"What now, Sir?"

I swallowed several times, trying to force saliva back into my dry mouth.

"Back to the station. We'll set up road blocks and start a door-to-door. Did anyone see any vehicles arriving or leaving Elderton Manor? If they did, what were they? Where were they heading? Who was driving? God, why did Shepherd pick today to arrange to sort out his cottage?"

I gave Grayson the car keys as my hands were shaking and I didn't trust myself behind the wheel. I had let her down. If Browning had taken her then it was all my fault because I hadn't protected her. I had even removed her tail for the weekend as Shepherd and I were both around.

Back in the station I left Grayson organising the door-to-door enquiries while I phoned Simon to see if Shepherd was still with him. I needed the lad here.

"Simon, it's Mike Malone. Sorry to interrupt you but is Alan Shepherd still with you?"

"Alan? Sorry, Mike but he never turned up for his appointment. Should have been here at nine forty five."

"Have you heard from him?"

"No. I just assumed there was some emergency and he was needed."

"Thanks, Simon."

I put the phone down with shaking hands. Both Cat and Shepherd were missing!

"Grayson!"

"Sir?"

"We need to get back to Elderton Manor. Shepherd never turned up for his appointment at the solicitors. If he tried to stop Browning, he could be lying injured inside the house." I uttered a silent prayer, hoping that he had not been added to the body count.

Within twenty minutes we were back outside the Manor. The front door was locked, the windows were locked.

"Round the back, we'll force the door."

Grayson followed me. From inside we could hear the barking of the dogs, confused by all the noise that we were making. The back door was locked and bolted from inside. It looked a sturdy piece of wood; this was going to take all our strength.

"After three, Grayson."

Together we ran and shoulder-barged the door. Nothing!

"Again!"

A second attempt. Still not a movement. I rubbed my shoulder.

"It'll have to be a window."

Pulling my jacket sleeve over my hand, I put my fist through the conservatory window. Together Grayson and I carefully made a hole large enough for us to squeeze safely through. As we opened the interior door, the Labradors leapt upon us, tails wagging furiously. We pushed them to one side and locked them in the downstairs toilet.

"You look downstairs, and I'll take the upstairs."

The silence was deafening as I climbed the stairs. From the quick glance that I taken, the downstairs rooms seemed fine; no signs of a struggle or of violence. I reached the landing and opened the first door. I knew that this was the room that Shepherd had let Cat have. Inside, the pillow still had the indentation of her head upon it. Gently, I put out my hand to touch it; it was cold. The sheets were turned back as if she had just stepped out of bed. I looked around. Everything was neat and tidy – except her shoes and clothes were still there. The clothes that she had been wearing yesterday were lying over the back of a chair, and her shoes were beneath it, waiting for her to step back into them. I pulled open cupboards and drawers. Everything was in its place. There were no signs of a struggle; he must have drugged her just as he had done the Blacks and taken her elsewhere.

Leaving the room I went down the landing to Shepherd's room. Taking hold of the handle, I turned it and stopped, afraid of what I might find on the other side. Taking a deep breath, I opened the door. It was the same as Cat's room. His uniform was hanging on the front of the wardrobe. His sheets were also turned neatly back. No struggle. Browning must have drugged him too. He must have wanted him out of the way so that he could concentrate upon Cat. But why take him? Why not knock him out and just leave him?

"Nothing down here, Sir."

Grayson's voice echoed in the empty house. I went onto the landing and looked over the banister at him.

"He's taken both Cat and Shepherd. Get the team over here. I'm going to the Cutler's again."

"Yes, Sir."

As I drove down the High Street, my mind was in turmoil. Where would he have taken them? Hopefully the Cutlers could give me a clue.

Morris Cutler was serving when I entered the shop. I stood and waited, tapping my foot impatiently. As his customer left, he turned to me, beaming.

"D.I Malone. Twice in one day?"

"I need to speak to you and your wife urgently. It's about Armstrong."

Cutler took one look at my face, then came around the front of the counter and put the closed sign in the window.

"This way. Lily's in the back – she's baby-sitting for next door."

The lounge would normally have been a cheerful place, with its pink walls and floral curtains, but today I wasn't in the mood to appreciate such things. Lily Cutler was sitting on a battered brown sofa reading to a small child who was curled up on her knee. She stopped mid-sentence as I entered.

"Hello, D.I. Malone. Take a seat please."

I pulled a chair from beneath the dining table and sat down.

"Just sit and read quietly, Lucy, there's a dear."

She lifted the child off her knee and placed her on the floor by her feet. The little girl immediately opened her book and began to trace the pictures with her chubby little fingers, singing as she did so.

"Mrs Cutler, I need to speak to you about the man you know as Christopher Armstrong. Can you tell me anything about him? Anything at all?"

She looked at her husband who shrugged his shoulders.

"Jack phoned us before Jonathon's funeral and asked if the lad could stay with us. As he was a friend of Jack's, we said yes."

"What can you tell me about him?"

"What do you mean?"

"What did he talk about? What did he do? Anything?" I knew that I was raising my voice again. "I'm sorry for shouting, but it is very important that we find him."

Morris Cutler went and stood beside his wife.

"He was a quiet lad. He asked a few questions about the place." Lily Cutler sat in silence, allowing her husband to answer my questions.

"Had you seen him before, Mrs Cutler?"

"No."

"Did he go anywhere while he was here?"

"For a drink." Morris Cutler was taking control of the conversation again.

"How did he arrive?"

"He had hired a car."

"So as far as you know, he only went to the funerals and to the pub?"

"And out with Cat Browning."

"Apart from Cat, did you see him talking to anyone else while he was here?"

"Not that I can remember."

"Yes he did," Lily Cutler interrupted. "Don't you remember? At Jonathon's funeral he was talking to Tony Wood about buying barns for conversions?"

"Tony Wood – his farm is on the main road?"

"Not really," Bill replied, "You turn off at the Shell garage and it is about a mile and a half down the track. It was a profitable little farm in his father's day. Poor old Tony's not a natural farmer. Lots of his land has gone to pasture."

"So, apart from Tony Wood, he never contacted anybody else, on either visit?"

They shook their heads.

"Do you know if he met Tony Wood again at Helen's funeral?"

"Don't think so."

Suddenly I felt a hand on my knee. The little girl was standing beside me, staring up at me with big blue eyes. She grinned and pushed her book onto my knee.

"I'd love to read, sweetheart, but I've got to go." I patted her hand.

"Baa, Baa Back Sheep," she sang "Hav'u any wool?"

"Good girl, Lucy. Come and sit here with me again." Lily held out her arms and Lucy trotted back to her.

"Thanks for your time." I stood to leave, and Morris

moved towards the door, blocking my path.

"What is all this about, Mr Malone?"

"I can't say a lot at the moment, but, we have reason to believe that Christopher Armstrong is not who he says he is. Furthermore we believe him to be extremely dangerous. If he should return, say nothing to him, but call the station straight away. Do nothing to make him suspicious."

Lily looked across at her husband and suddenly scooped Lucy up into her arms, protecting her.

"We will." Morris let me pass and at the shop door he took my arm. "But if he tries anything – well – I can look after my own, Mr Malone."

"I know you can, Morris. But hopefully it won't come to that."

Fifty Four

"It's here, Sir." Back at the station, Grayson had spread a map of the area over my desk. "This is Tony Wood's farm. There's only one way to it. Turn off the main road at the Shell garage and follow the road for about a mile and a half."

"What do you know of the farm?"

"Tony has let it go to ruin."

"Outhouses, barns? Are they easily accessible? Would Tony be able to see anyone going to and from them?"

"I don't think so. From what I can remember, you drive into the yard and the house is set back. I don't think that the outhouses nearest the lane can be seen from the house."

"So, Browning could be using them?"

"Are you sure this is where he is, Sir?"

"No. But this is the only lead I've got. So, could he be using them without Wood realising?"

"It's possible. I shouldn't think that Tony would be checking them. Rumour has it that he spends most of his time locked away with only a bottle of whisky for company, so I shouldn't think he bothers to check anything."

Memories of the whisky sodden Terry Hall floated to the front of my mind and I gave a passing thought to the plight of some farmers who were struggling to survive and failing.

"Right. Phone him and tell him to stay indoors and away from the barns."

Grayson left to make the phone call, and I studied the

map again. Looking at the farm's relationship to the village, it was so obvious. Easily reached, and far enough away from civilisation to allow Browning to come and go as he pleased without being noticed.

"No reply, Sir." Grayson joined us again around the map.

"OK – get the lads together – we're going over there."

I walked over to the crime-board and looked at the face of William Browning. Taking a pen, I drew a pair of dark glasses onto the photo. As soon as I had darkened hair, I saw the face of Christopher Armstrong staring back at me. I was furious. Why hadn't I spotted the similarity? I could even see the resemblance to Jonathon Black now, when it was too late. As I turned back to get my jacket, I remembered little Lucy standing next to me singing, and it hit me like a sledgehammer.

"Grayson! Grayson!" He came running back into the office. "It's Shepherd he's after, not Cat. All the time he has been after Shepherd,"

"Sorry, Sir?"

"Baa, Baa Black Sheep."

"Sir?" Grayson was looking at me incredulously as if I had taken leave of my senses.

"The nursery rhyme, 'Baa, Baa Black Sheep.' The black sheep is William Browning, born William Black."

Grayson was not following my line of thought at all.

"'One for the Master, one for the Dame'. Jonathon and Helen Black – the Master and the Dame."

"And 'the little boy who lives down the lane' is Shepherd?"

"Yes! And the 'three bags full' become three crates

full of wool. We've had two delivered to us, there has to be a third."

"Could be, Sir."

"So, why take Cat as well. That I don't understand. Where are those cars? It's possible that they may still be alive – after all he didn't kill the Blacks immediately."

Grayson left to check on the team. Reaching for my coat, I made my way to my own car. Outside four police cars were waiting for me to take the lead.

Fifty Five

He checked on the girl. Still out cold. Shepherd was beginning to stir, so he sat beside him and waited. He watched with some pleasure as Shepherd tried to stretch out his limbs, only to find them tightly bound. He watched him as he opened his eyes and looked around in panic, trying to find some normality in this abnormal situation in which he found himself. He watched as Shepherd's eyes, having become accustomed to the dim light, sought him out and widened in recognition. He watched him as his body tensed, as he fought against the ropes, his face reddening with the exertion of trying to spit out the gag. He watched, enjoying the spectacle of his captive struggling to escape and failing. He watched and said nothing.

Half an hour later we stopped at the top of the track. Cutting my engine, I got out and went over to the other cars.

"Right, lads, slow speed and no revving. Stop at the first barn and wait for my instructions."

The journey down towards the farm seemed to take forever. An owl rising from the ditch caused me to slam on my brakes; my nerves were in pieces. Fear of what Browning was doing to Shepherd and Cat was eating me up. Even on this cool afternoon, I could feel the sweat slowly trickling down my back.

As I turned the corner I saw the outline of the barn and stopped. Carefully shutting my door, I went to meet the others. We looked around us. There were two barns in the yard; I could see the farmhouse across the yard. Everything was still and lifeless and I hoped that this was not an omen.

"Split up. You four take the furthest barn. Grayson, and you two, come with me – and keep the noise down."

I watched the four men disappear around the corner before I gave the signal to my team. Slowly we made our way towards the nearest barn, keeping as close to the hedge as possible. There was not a sound to be heard; everything was as still as a grave. As soon as we reached the corner of the barn I raised my hand.

"You two go that way," I whispered. "Grayson and I will go this."

We watched the two constables inch their way around the edge of the barn and disappear. With a nod to Grayson we started to creep along the barn's wall. I had my face pressed against the wall as we moved, straining to hear sounds from within. Concentrating hard, I never even noticed the discarded farm implements at my feet until I hit them. I fell heavily. The sound of my fall upon the wooden handles echoed around the empty yard. Shit!

The sudden sound caused him to spin around, and he saw the light of hope glimmer in Shepherd's eye. He smiled, knowingly. Rising, he made his way to the barn door. Pressing his ear to the opening, he listened. From outside, the sound of someone scrambling to their feet drifted over to him. He would have to move quickly. He looked at the girl. Still unconscious. Swiftly, he made his way over to the corner of the barn where something lay hidden beneath a sheet of tarpaulin. He could see

*Shepherd watching his every move. Grasping the corner
of the tarpaulin, he looked over towards Shepherd and
watched him. He watched Shepherd's expression change
as with a flick of his wrist, he removed the sheet with the
same flair with which a magician removes his cloak
before the grand finale. He watched Shepherd's
expression register terror as he saw the crate waiting to
receive him; he had already placed the fleeces within the
crate to provide a nice, soft resting place. He watched as
Shepherd tried to twist himself onto his feet, as he kicked
against the ropes that were holding him, as he strained
so much that the tendons in his neck became taut. He
watched as Shepherd rolled over. He watched as
Shepherd's feet connected with an empty feed drum,
sending it clattering to the ground.*

I heard the sound of something falling within the barn.
"Grayson! They're inside."
My ankle was sore; I had twisted it when I had fallen.
Adrenaline was coursing through my body as Grayson
and I ran towards the barn doors.
"After three!"
We charged the door and it shuddered beneath our
weight and remained shut.

*He turned on his heels as he heard them attempt to
force the door. He could see Shepherd beginning to
relax, beginning to think that salvation was at hand. He
could see the girl beginning to stir. The door shuddered
again. He had to act. Now. He had so wanted to enjoy
this one, his final one. He had wanted to take his time*

and take pleasure in the act. No time. Taking a knife
from his pocket, he looked at Shepherd and smiled.

I looked around. There had to be something lying
around that I could use to open the door. I saw the two
constables appear around the corner and beckoned them
over.

"All four of us should do be able to it. After three."

We charged. There was a deafening crash and the
doors swung open.

"Stop! Police!"

Browning was a couple of feet away from Shepherd
and a knife was glinting in the dim light. Cat was curled
up in the corner and I could see her moving. They were
both alive. But, they weren't safe.

"Put the knife down!"

Browning stared at me, smiling. He took a step
backwards. A step closer to Shepherd.

"Put the knife down!"

Grayson and the others were behind me. I gave
Grayson a nod and he cautiously made his way over to
Cat. Browning's eyes never left my face. He was still
smiling.

"Why?" I asked.

He took another step backwards. If he moved quickly
he would be on the lad and there was nothing I could do.

"I asked you why? The lad isn't a Black. Why him?"

Browning continued to smile, but said nothing. I
nodded to Miller and Brooks, the two constables with
me. Slowly they inched away from me to try to make
their way up the sides of the barn, towards Shepherd.

233

Browning was still watching me.

"He took my place. They treated him like a son. It should have been me!" He was shouting. "I was their nephew. It should have been me!"

The smile had gone. It was like looking at a stage mask; cold, emotionless. He took another step backwards. I could see Brooks and Miller getting closer, but not close enough.

He watched the stupid policeman. He watched his face trying hard to be calm and reassuring. He watched the fear in his eyes as he took another step closer to Shepherd. Why should this greying policeman care what happened to Shepherd? He wasn't related. But he cared. He thought back over his life. Had anyone ever cared for him in this way? Bitterness rose in him like lava in a volcano. His mother had given him away. The man who adopted him, the man he had loved as a father, he had deserted him for that slut in the corner. No! No one had ever cared for him. No one ever would. He took another step closer to Shepherd and watched, without emotion, as the stupid policeman struggled to remain calm.

"Put the knife down!"

I was shouting. Panic was washing over me. Browning was standing over Shepherd. There was no way I could reach him. Brooks and Miller were too far away. I was powerless. He could do what he wanted and I couldn't stop him. I was aware of Shepherd at Browning's feet, trussed up like a pig ready for slaughter. I wanted to look at the lad. I wanted to give him some comfort. But I couldn't! I did not want to take my eyes from Browning. Not for a moment. He was watching me coldly. Suddenly, he took a deep breath and smiled as he raised the knife.

It happened so quickly. Shepherd had been at his mercy. He had won! He had defeated them all. He had been so busy watching that stupid policeman, that he hadn't seen Shepherd twisting his body. He hadn't seen Shepherd as with one movement, he had whipped his legs from under him.

Browning's fall had taken me by surprise and I had frozen. Browning was lying face down across the lad. I could see blood spreading across the dusty concrete floor, but I didn't know whose blood. I rushed over to Shepherd and kneeling beside him, I pulled the gag from his mouth.

"Get him off me!" he shouted.

Brooks and Miller lifted Browning clear and immediately I could see the knife. Browning had fallen with such force that the knife had been buried up to its hilt in his chest.

"He's dead, Sir." Miller said.

As I helped Shepherd out of his ropes, I turned and could see that Cat had already been released and was sitting in Grayson's jacket. He had his arm around her protectively. She was crying. As I smiled at her, I was relieved to see a weak smile in return. I turned my attention back to Shepherd.

"Nearly there, lad."

Miller had already left the barn to call for the team.

"Thank you, Sir." Shepherd was rubbing his wrists. His face was deathly pale; he looked so young and vulnerable. "How did you find me? Last night you were scrabbling in the dark – today you turn into the bloody cavalry."

"A lucky break. Browning's luck finally deserted him and came our way. How are you feeling?"

"Sore. How's Cat?"

"Let's go and see."

Helping him to his feet, we crossed the barn. Cat stood up and hugged us both. She was shivering.

"Come on, kids. Let's get you both back home."

"Yes, Dad!" Shepherd smiled gratefully at me. Giving him my coat, I led the way back to my car and piled them into the back seat. I was just opening my door when Grayson called me. He had gone to check the farmhouse.

"Sir, you need to come here."

I turned back to Shepherd and Cat, "I'll be back in a mo."

Walking over to Grayson, my ankle was throbbing. I would need to get that strapped as soon as I got back to the station.

"In here, Sir. We now know why Wood hadn't spotted Browning."

He opened the back door of the farmhouse and the smell caused me to step backwards. Taking a handkerchief from my pocket, I covered my nose and mouth and went in. The buzzing of the flies was deafening. Browning must have killed Tony Wood soon

236

after Jonathon Black's funeral. The poor chap had been lying here ever since. I had seen enough.

"The team can sort that out. I'm taking the kids home, and then I'll meet you back at the station."

Once outside I took a deep breath and closed my eyes, trying to erase the image of the rotting corpse in the kitchen. Getting into the car, I said nothing. They didn't need to know. Not yet.

Fifty Six

For the third time within a month I was standing in a graveyard. The difference was that there were only two mourners to watch as this coffin was laid to rest. Elizabeth Summers and her husband. There was no sign of David Browning, no sign of the father who had broken a little boy's heart, no sign of the man who had taken away a little boy's capacity for love and replaced it with capacity for hate. Unable to look upon Elizabeth Summers' grief a moment longer, I left the churchyard and made for my car.

Turning out of the churchyard, I set my nose towards home and the meal that Cat and Shepherd were cooking for me. They had not quite put the events of the past few days behind them, but they were getting there. They had certainly become a lot closer. I was glad, they were both good kids.

And what about me? Some of the doors in my mind had been opened and old memories had walked through my thoughts, some bringing pain, some bringing laughter. Now all of those doors were closed again. The past was safely locked away again until such a time as I was able to walk hand-in-hand with it in the sun. I had wanted a bombshell to wake up this sleepy little place and it certainly had done. Unfortunately, the debris from its explosion was going to linger in our minds and bodies for months. Rest and recuperation was what we all needed now. And good food!

Cat and Shepherd had told me that the menu for tonight was going to be a surprise. It had better not be

238

lamb!

ABOUT THE AUTHOR

Milly Reynolds lives in Lincolnshire with her husband, son and two cats. Until recently Milly was a full-time English teacher, but she has now left the profession to devote time to her writing.

Living in Lincolnshire, Milly loves its flat, endless landscapes and tries to incorporate these into her novels. She also has a passion for all forms of crime fiction which was why she decided to create her own 'hero' – Mike Malone. Rather than wanting to compete with the masters of the genre, she made the decision that Mike Malone would be more off-beat; she wants her novels to have humour in them. She wants to make readers chuckle rather than scream.

The Woolly Murders is the first in a series of Mike Malone Mysteries.

Printed in Great Britain
by Amazon

17108818R00139